Constructed

To Last

Brianna Casey

Contents

Content & Trigger Warnings

Sexual Content 18+
Explicit Language
Severe Anxiety
Body Dysmorphia
Body Shaming
Alcohol Abuse
Medical Content
Sudden Loss

Disclaimer:
None of the characters or places within this novel
are accurate representations of any one individual
or place,
all persons created are fictional and purely for
entertainment purposes only.

Dedication

To my son, my family, my friends, and my readers.
Thank you.

Dedication

Prologue

BAILEY

It's 7:30 pm, and instead of heading into the house, I'm captivated by the thunder rolling above, and the large rain drops tapping off the windshield of my gray Toyota Camry.

It's early spring in Colorado, my favorite time of the year aside from autumn. The gentle chill in the air, a reminder that it's not yet summer, is complemented by the absence of ice on the roads, a clear sign that winter has finally passed. I'm not a huge fan of ice and snow, despite the fact that I choose to stay in Colorado even as an adult.

It's not until the rain comes to a halt and I start to yawn that I look down at my phone to see it's nearing nine pm. Reluctantly, I grab my messenger bag, keys, phone, and now empty coffee cup and push open the drivers side door.

I'm hit with the smell of fresh rain and wet grass. My long wavy auburn hair is swept across my face by the wind, twirling up and around into itself, most likely creating a knot that will be fun to brush out later.

I ascend the steps and unlock the door to the two-bedroom I share with my friend and coworker, Aspen. Upon entering, I place my bag on the round, two-person breakfast table, toss my cup in the trash, and collapse onto the weathered brown leather couch in our living room.

My 40 pound, mostly white with splotches of brown Australian Shepherd is sleeping peacefully. She was born deaf, so it's not until she feels my weight shifting to the cushion she's sleeping on that alerts her of my presence.

Her piercing blue eyes flutter open, and she thrusts her tongue straight onto my face, greeting me with a frenzied tail wag that nearly topples a lamp from the table beside the couch.

After a few gentle passes along her silky back and kisses on her long snout, I rise to retrieve her harness and leash. Aspen had let her out when she returned home from work a few hours ago, but I'm certain she'll enjoy another quick walk before bed.

We live in a two story duplex, and there's twelve homes here split between three separate buildings. Most of the neighbors have been here for at least a decade; I'm one of the newer residents only having been living here with Aspen for a few months.

Nestled away from the nearest major city and with a good 30 acres of land surrounding us, we enjoy the tranquility of nature, uninterrupted by any other buildings. The stars are bright and the sky is clear of pollution, it's utter perfection if you don't mind living the slow life.

The only other structure nearby is a single charming pumpkin farm, about five miles up a dirt path that adds to the picturesque ambiance. During the fall season, it transforms into a popular place for Halloween festivities featuring a haunted house, zombie paintball, and a cute petting zoo for the little ones. The owners are sweet and make it so incredibly special, that families from the city will drive up to partake in the events as well.

Our immediate neighbors Sandy and Rob, whom we share a wall with, is a wonderful couple in their late 60's and as vibrant as can be.

I see Sandy through their living room blinds as we pass by, sitting in her favorite chair reading a book, cozied up with a thick quilt she crafted herself.

She's most likely reading one of her frisky romance novels with Fabio on the cover that she shamelessly loves, and Rob not so shamelessly loves to tease her for.

If she doesn't have a book in her hand, she's busy in the kitchen making Rob's favorites, or chatting on the phone with one of her children or many friends.

She notices me quickly, tipping her reading glasses down the bridge of her nose, and gives me a brilliant smile and a gentle wave.

There's a photo of them on her coffee table from their early 30's. She had medium length pitch black hair, stunning blue eyes that radiate her kindness, and the flashiest smile. Beautiful inside and out, even to this day though her hair is now gray and her eyes are more dull in color.

In the photo, Rob is glancing down at his wife with a shy and loving smile, dark slicked back hair, and a face of a person that you can see immediately is gentle and kind. You can witness their deep love for each other, both now and then.

Every time I look at the cherished memory captured within the silver frame, I can't help but wonder if I'll ever have a photo like that gracing my coffee table, and I carry this thought with me as I head inside and off to my bedroom.

I slip into some cozy pajamas, gather my hair into a bun, brush my teeth, and settle into my queen-sized bed draped in my thick, white comforter.

Echo immediately jumps up and settles snugly against my back as I lie on my side facing the window. I rescued her when I moved here, but really I feel like she rescued me. My family was worried about my transition back here alone, and said they would feel better if I had a companion. She's my soul dog and a stage five clinger. Downright obsessed with me, as I am her.

The rain starts pouring down again, and I decide to skip turning on the box fan that's resting against my dresser on the floor, facing the bed. I usually need the white noise from the fan to sleep, but tonight, the crackling thunder and the pitter-patter of rain against the tin roof of the shed outside will lull me to sleep.

Chapter One

BAILEY

The day I met Rylan Sterling marked the beginning of my life, I just refused to acknowledge it for a while because of course, I'm a female and that's what we do apparently.

To be fair, he didn't pay any attention to me at first either. He was distracted by a phone call that had his jaw tense and brows furrowed.

"Dark Roast. Large. Black." He barked at me under his breath with one hand covering the mouthpiece of his phone. No please, no thank you, barely even glancing in my direction.

"What an ass," I whisper through the private channel of the headset to Aspen.

"Yeah, a hot piece of ass." She replies, gawking in his direction.

Sure, if you like toxic masculinity.

As I wait for a fresh pot of coffee to brew for said ass, I couldn't help but notice that Aspen was right. *He is hot.*

Ridiculously hot.

With a huff he shifts his well over 6 foot frame against the condiment bar, and pushes back his dark brown hair that falls in front of his eyes.

He's not extremely muscular by any means, but he's far from lanky and it's easy to see through his pressed suit that he spends some time in the gym.

His thick hair has a slight wave to it, and looks unkept but styled like that intentionally, and I wonder if it would look as good slicked back by my hand.

His mesmerizing hazel eyes, reminiscent of the leaves that fall off our local trees in autumn, are striking. I mean, this man is beautiful. Where did he come from and are there more like him? He looks very displaced in our small mountain town.

Aspen snaps me out of my daydreaming, "Earth to Bailey! Coffee is ready!"

She giggles and elbows my side, "Whatcha thinking about?"

I brush past her to pour the coffee and reply in a hushed playful tone,

"Oh, just how much I'd like to climb him like a tree."

I can make jokes like this with her, but my confidence is lacking far too much to act on anything.

Placing his to-go cup on the bar, I call out his order and slide off to the side to watch him from behind the safety of the espresso machine like a stalker.

As he approaches the bar, he shoves his phone into his pocket. His right hand reaches up to stroke his trimmed beard, which frames his sharp jawline. His left hand reaches for the coffee. There's no ring on his finger, which suggests he's not married. If his interaction with me is any indication of his personality, this is not a huge shock. Attractiveness can only get you so far.

He briskly heads out of the shop to sit out on the outdoor patio. Unfortunately, I'm unable to continue watching him as business begins to pick up, and it isn't until a few weeks later that I would see him again.

I've always been a bit of an outsider, and I've never had more than a couple close friends here and there throughout the years growing up.

I was born and raised in a small farming town in California, then came here to Elk Hollow when I was thirteen.

My parents chose to wait until us kids were finished with high school before relocating, and when I was twenty-two, they retired and moved to Denver where my mom could pursue her dream of owning her own art studio.

I chose to move with them, hoping I could find my purpose there as well and attempted night classes at a local college while working full time at Starbucks for a few years.

I only managed to get my associates within that time and decided to stop waisting money on school when I had no idea what I wanted to do with my life.

I then got a job at a health food market that paid more, and there I found myself a part of a small friend group. Though it wasn't long before my first mature relationship ended horribly, and caused the rest of my ties to the group to fall apart.

One of the girls in the group, Liz, who worked in the freezer department began sleeping with my boyfriend Anthony, who was a front end manager like myself.

I wasn't too surprised given the fact that I wasn't willing to sleep with him after almost six months of being exclusive. Lizzie on the other hand was more than happy to throw her tits at him in my place during an overnight shift that *apparently* didn't require much work.

I'm not one to slut shame, but that was low.

Anyways, this made it very easy for me to quit my job after two years, and return to Elk Hollow, population roughly 350.

I'm pretty shy and reserved on average, and I've never thought too highly of myself. It doesn't help that I'm about 220 pounds at only 5'4".

When I landed the job at Brews N Booze, I befriended Aspen. More accurately, she befriended me, and I went with it. She is radiant, lively, and full of energy. Anyone who meets her, loves her immediately; even though she can be a tad overbearing for the average recluse at first.

Fortunately for me, she had an empty room that she insisted I take. Since I was still living in the only motel just outside town, it would've been ridiculous for me to decline her offer.

As I was moving in, one of the boxes containing a portion of my book collection unexpectedly came apart and spilled out in front of our duplex. Sandy, who was sitting outside in her rocking chair with a cup of black coffee and a blueberry muffin, promptly stood to help me. It was during this moment that we discovered our shared love for romance novels, and I offered to let her borrow a book that she appeared to be interested in. From that moment on, our friendship was forever sealed.

Aspen and Sandy are my only two friends here, and honestly, I'm okay with that. It's two more friends than I would've had if I had stayed with my family in Denver. Which is surprising considering the population there is much higher.

My mother Dana, a retired teacher and artist runs her dream art studio downtown, and my Father Bradley, a retired psychologist that loves to spend his days wherever my mother is, met in Kindergarten and I swear they have the perfect love story.

My brother Alec and his wife Becca met in high school, and their relationship appears to be nauseatingly perfect as well. I may sound a bit bitter, but I genuinely love them and am happy for them and their successes.

Alec works for a prestigious law firm downtown, while Becca is a NICU nurse at the Children's Hospital. Their first home is a charming three-story townhouse with a spacious yard, which is ideal for raising a family.

And then there's me, a 27-year-old college dropout who has no clue how to be an adult. I work as a barista in our local coffee shop by day- bar by night, and I'm still trying to figure out who I am and what I want in life. I feel like I'm just drifting through existence.

All I need right now is my dog and my books. At this pace, I'm probably going to end up as a 40-year-old dog lady. How do I sign up for that?

I pull into the parking lot for my midday shift, and for a fleeting moment, I'm reminded of the enigmatic man with mesmerizing hazel eyes, impeccably tailored suit, and a deep commanding voice. I can't help but assume that he's a successful businessman with a meticulously planned future similar to Alec, definitely on a different level than I am.

In the coffee industry, customers are often rude until they take their first sip of caffeine. One would expect them to be more excited knowing that their preferred stimulant is about to enter their system, but that's not always the case, unfortunately.

I remember one time in particular when I was working as a a shift lead in Denver, a customer threw a breakfast sandwich through the window at my barista, it was her first week and this was her first job. I felt so sorry for the girl, and I absolutely demanded the customer drive off without a refund or replacement.

Fortunately, we don't encounter issues like that in Elk Hollow. Everyone here knows each other and genuinely cares for one another.

The most significant problem I've had with a customer here was when a trailer came unlatched in the parking lot, and before we even knew what was happening, a horse came walking through the rolling patio door that opens into the shop. The horse made its way through the pastry case far too quickly for us to take action, and ate everything inside of it.

If I'm being completely honest with myself, my dream is to one day open up my own cozy coffee shop, one that preferably doesn't have an alcohol bar attached to it. But instead, a vibrant library with one of those sliding ladders and deep cozy chairs

placed strategically throughout the shop. I can picture it clear as day, and the thought of having that
become a reality someday brings me a tinge of
excitement.

Knowing that my dream is unlikely to become
a reality though, I don't typically allow myself to
indulge or dwell on it too often.

However, today seems like an ideal day for some
daydreaming.

Chapter Two

RYLAN

"You've got to be kidding me, Ky! You know how uncomfortable meetings like this make me. Now you aren't even going to show up?" I could wring my brothers neck I think to myself as I wait for him to respond on the other end.

I'm sitting in my rental car outside of the coffee shop in the middle of bum fuck nowhere.

Brews N Booze - hmm, can't say I've seen something like this before. I wonder if 8 AM is too early for a brew, and seriously contemplate ordering one if they serve them this early. It's 5 o'clock somewhere, right?

My brother Kyle and I work for our father, who owns a substantial real estate investment firm. My current task is to finalize a contract for a new strip mall that will begin construction soon. Initially, we were scheduled to attend this meeting together, but unfortunately, they have prioritized other matters and have since delegated the responsibility to me without my knowledge.

"Ry, Dad is meeting with McMann in Los Angeles tomorrow morning to go over the details on the new hotel, and I've got a Skype meeting with Mr. Hamasaki from Japan tonight at eleven. Don't make this personal." My brother huffed while rustling some papers around.

I can hear his secretary, Amy, in the background, diligently rattling off his schedule for the day. I find it hard to comprehend how she has managed to work for him for the past five years. Despite being a genuinely kind and caring woman with a husband and children whom she rarely sees due to Kyle's demanding schedule, the amount of time and dedication she has invested into my brother, I don't believe he is even aware of her family. This is the sole reason I have chosen not to hire a secretary for myself. I am determined not to put anyone else through the bullshit if I can help it.

"I've got a lot going on here." Kyle takes a deep breath and whispers something to Amy that I can't quite make out.

"Call Dad, bitch at him. He's the one who scheduled these meetings."

And with that, silence. Asshole hung up on me. I know he was aware of these changes before I took a company jet out here alone, and he didn't have the courtesy to give me a heads up.

I like to be behind the scenes, not meeting with clients. My brother is much better with this kind of thing. He's got a stick up his ass all the time, and often comes across as a bully. He gets things done and doesn't take shit from anyone. Unlike me, who caves under pressure. I don't like conflict and I've been accused of being altruistic, which apparently is not a favorable trait to have when doing business.

Kyle is going to take over once Dad retires, we all know it, and I'm perfectly okay with it. I make more than enough money in my current sitting position, and I have no desire to be head of the company regardless of the pay raise. I'm a simple man, and I take pleasure in the mundane. Flashy is not my preference, but it's definitely Kyle's and he thrives off of this lifestyle.

I decide I might as well get some coffee to help get me through this phone call with my father. The lead contractor won't be here for another half hour, which will give me time to have this uncomfortable conversation and gulp down a cup.

I slide out of my rented black Nissan Altima and make my way into the coffee shop. Just as I approach the counter to order, I feel my phone vibrate in my pocket. Dad. Reluctantly I answer, knowing if I ignore his call it would only upset him.

"I was just informed that you are unhappy with the responsibility I've left you with. I'm sorry to disappoint but I am relying on you to get this done for us. It is a very important deal I need closed, I trust you can do this without a hitch?"

I sigh, turns out he's already upset, maybe I should've ignored the call after all.

I feel even worse for my fathers secretary Delores, which I'm assuming is the person who retained the information about my chat with Kyle, through poor Amy. Now, Delores, she's got one foot in the ground, and has been with my dad since the beginning. She doesn't tolerate any disrespect, not even from my father. The woman is an angel, and I'm certain she wouldn't have aged as rapidly if she hadn't continued working for him.

I put my hand up to my phone so I can order quickly before answering his question.

"Dark Roast. Large. Black." I whip out my card and hold it to the reader then walk away to finish the conversation in private.

"Of course, but you could've at least warned me that I would be doing this on my own, I feel wildly underprepared for this meeting. Why did you choose this location anyway?"

I'm growing more uncomfortable in this suit the longer I'm in it. I only dress formal when I'm forced to, and I find myself continuously shifting to make room for my body as there is absolutely no give to this material. He's put me on hold and my patience is growing thin when I hear "Large black coffee on the bar!" being called out.

"I already have some potential buyers lined up and I think it's a great investment for the companies future. Just close this deal, and send over the confirmation once you get settled in. I'll see you in a couple of months." Silence, again.

A couple of months, settled in? What the hell is that supposed to mean? I quickly stuff my phone back into my pocket and retrieve my liquid gold from the bar. Once outside, I find a table to sit at while I wait for the contractor, and pull my phone back out to check my email. I immediately see an updated itinerary that Delores had typed out for me while I was on the flight.

"Fuck." I whisper under my breath.

They expect me to stay here until the job is finished and depending on the project's size, that could take up to a year. I start gulping down my coffee and close my eyes. What on earth am I supposed to do here for an entire year?

Chapter Three

RYLAN

The meeting with the contractor yesterday went surprisingly well, even though I was under-prepared, overwhelmed, and overall in a terrible mood. I've screwed up several business contracts in the past. Not because I'm not intelligent enough to do business; it's because I'm too accommodating, or 'soft,' as my father would so eloquently put it. My tendency to compromise on timeframes and budgets to make the other party feel more satisfied or comfortable often ends up costing the firm and our clients significantly more than we anticipate.

By the grace of God, or whoever, yesterday went exactly as my father had meticulously planned. Things are set in motion to begin the next steps which lead me closer to being back home. Home; a midsize high-rise loft apartment in Dallas, Texas.

My older Brother Kyle, my older sister Rachel, me, and our baby sister Natasha were raised in The Woodlands by our parents Adam and Patricia.

Kyle, the eldest at thirty-eight, married to his work and naturally feels responsible for the three of us. As a result, he's always been the mature one.

Rachel, thirty-six, being the first daughter has always felt the need to prove she can live up to the pedestal she was put on as a child.

Then there's Daniel, Rachel's spouse of eight years. Faithful husband, dedicated lawyer at the firm, and a good father to their three children.

Reyna was born first, she's seven. Then came Jack, he's five. And their newest addition Allison is almost one. Cute kids, very polite and proper of course.

I haven't spent much time with them outside of business events, charities, and holidays, but I can tell their parents are grooming them to be mini work horses and trophy wives to continue on the Sterling legacy.

Next down the line of Sterling children is me, Rylan Caine. Thirty-one, no spouse or girlfriend, or even a pet. Which I suppose is a relief in the moment considering I'm going to be away from home for the foreseeable future.

I graduated at the top of my class at Texas A&M with a masters degree in Business administration, just like my brother Kyle. Not exactly what I wanted for myself, but it's a career choice that was handed to me the moment I began Kindergarten.

Lastly, our beautiful wallflower sister, Natasha. At just twenty-two, she's the youngest and fiercely unapologetically herself.

She doesn't have a college degree or a career. Instead, she has her art, and her boyfriend, Mikey. They travel together across the United States in their home on wheels, and they document their daily life adventures on social media with their Golden Doodle, Milo, and their one-eyed cat, Jones.

I wished many times that I could live a carefree life like my little sister, and I've always been jealous of her in some aspects. Despite my jealousy, I am very proud of her.

She didn't conform, and was able to see past the bullshit and realize the way her parents and older siblings were living, was not all there was to life. That's why she packed up and left with Mikey as soon as they graduated High School. She got the hell out of dodge before she could end up being tied down to something intertwined within the family.

Her boyfriend is a solid dude who I know will keep her safe and happy. She's my baby sister and it's my job to be protective over her, even if she could easily hold her own and take care of herself I'm sure.

My parents adore her, but they certainly don't understand her, or her willingness to distance herself from the Sterling family. Somehow, they don't see her as a disappointment though, but more of a *work in progress.*

They assume that she will eventually find her way back to them when she's ready. But Tash won't touch this life with a ten-foot pole.

May God bless her and her hippie spirit self.

My childhood was far from perfect, but it wasn't terrible either. Between summer camps, vacations, and private schools for all the Sterling children; we also had Gala's, business trips, board meetings, and fundraisers as we grew older.

Adam, our father, worked his way up the career ladder. Spending nights and weekends in the office paid off for the family before I could walk. He put in the time and proved himself worthy, and with that

Sterling & Sons Real Estate Investment Firm, aptly known as S&S, was born.

Long nights and weekends turned into long weeks away from home, but this allowed our mother Patricia to quit her day job as a secretary in a dental office, and she was finally able to stay home with us kids just like she had always wanted to. She provided us with a safe and mostly nurturing environment. Our father on the other hand is the strong arm. Quick to lay down the law, and announce his disappointments, particularly with us Sterling boys.

"You must live up to our family name. Don't you dare let me or your mother down," he would say whenever we deviated from the expected path he had laid out for us kids.

In my junior year of high school, I got into a fight with a senior quarterback because he was bullying a junior on the chess team. That was the last time I fought; my father made sure of it. He didn't care about the reason behind the fight, all he wanted was to prevent it from happening again.

Despite his overall good character at the time, prior to the full on corruption, my brother Kyle experienced a brief but intense mental breakdown during his college years that nearly jeopardized his degree. He had spent his entire childhood striving for perfection and once he finally gained independence, he snapped.

Fortunately, it was a misdemeanor that our father was able to have expunged from his school and personal record; it's evident that having financial resources and connections can have its advantages.

Unfortunately, once everything was restored to it's original state before the onset of his early midlife crisis, he transitioned to his full-blown Mr. Sterling Jr. persona. I can't recall the last time I witnessed my brother engage in any form of relaxation or form a genuine connection with anyone outside of his business dealings. Dad had certainly done a number on him.

These days our mother spends all of her time at the country club, or with my sister Rachel and the kids. Rachel is a stay at home mom on the PTA, a member of their neighborhood HOA, a volunteer at the local homeless shelter, and is also a troop leader for Reyna's Girl Scout troop. She's extremely involved in her kids' lives, as well as their community.

Rachel's depression spiked at an all time high after having Allison, something they called postpartum depression, and she seems to be just going through the motions these days. That's in part to why our mother spends so much of her time with Rachel and the kids. I think she worries that one day Rachel will pull a Britney Spears and shave her head or do something else crazy, that would ultimately shine a bad light on our family.

Daniel her husband, like dad, spends a minimum of 60 hours a week at the firm. But when he's home, he's tentative and present. If only the need to please his father in law, and make more money didn't mean as much to him.

It seems the only person I don't need to worry about is Tash. I think she's the only Sterling kid that's not completely fucked up in one way or another.

I should call her and see if she'll be anywhere near Colorado soon, I'm due for one of her hugs and insightful lengthy tangents about the true meaning of life and the pursuit of happiness. Or whatever it is that she's into these days.

Chapter Four

BAILEY

I spent the past three days visiting my parents in Denver with Echo and Aspen. It had been a while since I last visited, and I missed them and Alec quite a bit.

Luckily, Aspen and I were able to take the same days off from work this week. She was dying to spend some time in the city. If she had her way, she could shop for days without stopping. I can't even begin to count how many oddity shops and thrift stores we visited, and my car is so full that I'm slightly worried we won't be able to afford rent this month. Despite the clutter, we had a blast, making it all worthwhile.

On the first day, we had a peaceful evening, which was much needed after the five-hour drive. Naturally, my parents took an immediate interest in my love life and future plans. I understand they're concerned about me, and their prying wasn't out of disappointment or anything like that. Of course, I'm not Alec, but that doesn't bother them; they just want me to be happy. I think it bothers me more that I haven't been as successful, and don't have the same drive he does to be a productive member of society.

The following day, we had our shopping spree downtown and ended the evening with a loud dinner with my parents, Alec, his wife Becca, and a few of their friends. On our final morning, we gathered for breakfast, then strolled through the busy local farmers market, where of course Aspen spent more money.

Next, we headed to Costco to stock up on household essentials before returning home.

While I don't miss living there, I do enjoy the time spent with my family, and the convenience of having big-box stores nearby.

Beep *Beep* *Beep*
The clock reads 4 AM. It should be illegal to open a coffee shop at 5 AM, considering that the same coffee shop was open until 1 AM as a bar.

Fortunately, it's prohibited to have an employee on staff for the coffee bar within the same 24-hour period as the alcohol bar, which eliminates the possibility of minimal breaks between shifts.

Unfortunately, Aspen covered the bar for a coworker last night, so her next shift at the shop won't be until tomorrow morning.

Consequently, I'll be short-staffed today. Which is freakin fantastic.

Hopefully, it'll be slow since it's a Tuesday, and nothing ever happens on Tuesdays, or any day for that matter, really.

I make sure to take Echo out for a long walk, and grab a bottled protein drink from the fridge before heading off to work.

My long curly brunette hair is put into a lazy top bun with some strands framing my face this morning, and the only makeup I felt like putting on was some black mascara that makes my blue eyes pop. My eyes are by far my favorite feature about myself, that and my dimples. I didn't like them as a child, but I've grown to appreciate them as an adult.

I flip my visor down, double-checking my hair and makeup in the vanity mirror. Once I'm satisfied, I flip the visor back up and glance at the clock on the dash. I have five minutes to kill before I need to head inside the building to open up. I don't expect to see a customer for at least thirty minutes or more, no one ever comes in when we first open.

It's then that I spot a black car with heavily tinted windows parked out front which is a little unnerving. I didn't notice it when I pulled in and the only other business within this lot, Elk Hollow bank, doesn't open up for another two hours. I'm the only one expected to be anywhere around here right now.

Most of the locals up at this time are doing farm chores and won't be indulging in take out caffeine for another few hours, and none of them drive a brand new sedan.

As I approach the front door, I fiddle with the shop keys and discretely keep my gaze fixed on the Nissan in the lot; trying not to appear overly nervous or obvious in my stare.

Just as I turn to reach for the open sign, I notice that the man inside the car has lowered the window enough for me to catch a glimpse of his face. To my horror, it's the asshole in the suit. Now, I can't deny that I feel like a stalker, and I'm certain he's aware that I'm watching him closely. Alternatively, he could be a creep. I mean, what is he doing out there this early in the morning?

Oh right.. we serve coffee. That's probably what he's wanting, Bailey. You listen to too many true crime podcasts I think to myself.

Behind the counter, I clock in and begin grinding whole beans. Once I'm done, I put on my headset, start the espresso machines, brew the first pot, and head to the back to retrieve a cash drawer from the safe.

As I return to the front of house through the swinging cafe door, I'm startled by a figure standing directly in front of me. I let out a yelp and quickly grab the cash drawer to prevent it from falling and spilling out everywhere.

"Shit! You scared me!" I squeak out breathlessly.

The man chuckles and quickly apologizes.

"I'm sorry, that wasn't my intention. The sign says you open at five and I'm in desperate need of a fix," He gestures to the store hours sign on the front door.

"My motel room has the worst coffee I've ever had the displeasure of tasting. Really, it should come with a warning label."

Hmm, motel room. That explains why I've never seen him before. We only have one motel right outside of town, think Bates Motel. It's the one I lived in for a few weeks before moving in with Aspen, and I can confirm, the coffee is practically on par with sewer water.

"Dark roast, right?" I blurt out before realizing how creepy it is for me to remember this man's order.

God, he's wearing grey sweatpants, a black t-shirt, and a black zip-up hoodie with sneakers.

Despite his casual attire, he still looks just as handsome as he did when I first saw him. I swear I can see his pecks through his hoodie, and his bulge through his sweats. Oh, is it getting hot in here? Must. Look. Away.

"Yeah... that's right? Do I just give off the impression that's what I drink or is that all you have ready right now?" He asks with almost an offended tone.

Of course he doesn't remember me.

"No? I believe I took your order last week,"

I know I shouldn't keep going, but I can't help myself. It's early, he startled me, and he wasn't exactly the nicest person during our first run in.

"But why would you remember me? You were too busy with your phone and your head up your ass to notice anything or anyone else around you. It's glaringly obvious that you're not from around here."

Well, that actually felt pretty good, and I have no shame. Zero. Until I notice his lip curl and his beautiful eyes soften.

"I'm sorry." He says gently. Reaching up to run his fingers through his hair, he looks up at me briefly and then back down to his hands holding his wallet almost as if he's too ashamed to look me in the eyes.

"I'm not usually like that, it was a rough morning, and you're right. I was in my own little bubble and I'm not from around here."

Damn. I wasn't expecting that, now I feel like an asshole for pointing it out.

"It's fine," I say sharply as I reach for a large cup to pour his freshly brewed coffee into.

"Sorry I called you out for being a dick. Welcome to Elk Hollow, coffee's on me this morning."

I turn and start walking towards the back room without looking back, "Just, don't leave a bad review. I kind of need this job and it's one of five places to work at in town."

Within seconds of disappearing, I hear the ding of the front door indicating he's gone. Phew, that was awkward. I'm awkward. At least with locals I know what I'm going to get.

Hopefully he doesn't say anything to the owner, she likes me but it's not going to look great regardless if he's an outsider just passing through or not.

Elk Hollow is growing and we're all learning to adapt, sooner or later the town could be so large that we begin to attract tourists. It is beautiful up here, and our little town is so aptly named after the fact we had more elk residents than human residents when it was officially founded 30 years ago.

The middle school and high school are combined with how few students we have here, and there were only 20 kids in my graduating class.

The mayor mentioned at our last town hall that some buyers have shown interest, and to prepare for more business' and homes going up within the next few years. I'm really hoping it doesn't pan out and that the buyers drop out. There's a reason we all love it here, and that includes the lower population.

However, it would be nice to have a Target.

Chapter Five

RYLAN

Day eight of being confined to this motel room, and I'm utterly bored out of my fucking mind. Everything is beyond walking distance, and it takes more than half an hour to drive into town from here.

Elk Hollow is the smallest town I've ever been to.

Upon arriving, you'll notice the 'Welcome to Elk Hollow - Population: More Elk Than People' sign. Just 15 miles down the road, you'll come across the 'See Ya Later!' sign.

It's only current business' are a gas station that doubles as a diner, a firehouse police station that's single-handedly run by Captain Johnston and a few volunteers, two schools, a coffee shop/bar hybrid, a mom and pop grocery store, Elk Hollow Bank, and a single-screen movie theater attached to a laundromat. The only gym in town is located within the middle school-high school combination, that fortunately is open to the public during off-hours.

There's ample land here, and most residents reside on the outskirts of town. It feels like I've been transported to Riverdale, complete with Archie, Betty, Jughead, and Veronica.

The grocery store is a gem, as it stocks all local produce, meat, eggs, and milk. However, the downside to my current situation is that I lack a kitchen to prepare any of that in.

I pull open my laptop and connect to my hotspot, needing to find a rental if I'll be out here as long as Delores scheduled me for.

Listing : FOR RENT.
Two bed, two full bath, one half bath.
Full kitchen, washer and dryer hookup, living and dining area with breakfast bar.
Pets allowed, non smoking. Two story duplex.
Price : $3,200/month.

Perfect, a fully equipped kitchen and laundry hookup were my top priorities. A person can only eat so many hamburgers and milkshakes before suffering some sort of cardiac event. Plus, it's only a twenty-minute drive from the heart of town. Soon, I'll be required to be on-site daily to oversee the construction, and these winding back roads are sketchy after dark.

I'm also considering getting a different vehicle when I drive back down the mountain. The sedan was suitable for a short visit, but if I'll be staying up here for the winter, I'll need an SUV or pickup with four-wheel drive. Dallas doesn't experience significant snowfall, so I'm not particularly experienced in driving through blizzards on top of a mountain.

When I brought the company jet to Colorado, I had to drive another four hours up to reach my final destination, which was not what I was expecting. I will say, the drive was surreal. I've never seen a more beautiful sight the further away from the city I got. And here I am, fucking it all up in my fathers name. Sure, maybe someday the town would've grown, but why did we have to be the ones taking the first shot at it?

I submit my application for the rental and close my laptop when I notice my stomach growling. One in the afternoon and I haven't had anything to eat. I should get in the shower and head down to the diner for a quick meal. Tomorrow I'll get a new vehicle and hopefully by then, I'll hear back about the duplex.

"Rylan, I assume everything is on track since we haven't heard from you? I've been trying to reach you all morning."

Driving down the stretch of highway, I take note that it's only seven and my phone has a single bar of service.

I left the motel an hour ago to get a head start on dropping off the Altima, and picking up a truck I bought last night from a Toyota dealer in Denver.

After that, I need to stop at an appliance store to order some things for the duplex I move into tonight.

I'm under a lot of pressure, and my father is only concerned with one thing; which isn't how I'm handling this transition.

"Sorry, I've been on the road, a little busy trying to get comfortable since I will be here for the foreseeable future." I say with a slightly irritated tone that I hope he doesn't catch on to.

"Your brother and I are leaving for Japan tomorrow. See to it that everything runs smoothly on your end." Silence.

Something I've grown accustomed to over the years. Why say goodbye when it was barely a two way conversation?

I open Spotify and resume my true crime podcast, and take a sip of the dreadful motel coffee as I watch the scenery zip past me.

Texas may have its charm, but this view is unparalleled.

I miss my friends and the comfort of my home, but this place? This is where I could envision myself living someday.

I have a couple more hours to Denver, and I can't help but think about the duplex with a small sense of excitement.

I haven't seen it in person yet, but it was the only available place, and I'm fortunate enough to have the financial means to afford it.

I'm fully aware of my financial situation and don't take it for granted, but I also tend to live modestly.

According to the owner Jake, it had been sitting empty for a while now, and he was going to list it for sale if there wasn't a renter before summer.

The views from the duplex that I could see online are stunning, and I think I'll feel a lot less stressed about this situation once I'm in a better routine.

I'm also contemplating taking a weekend to return home and grab some things that will enhance my comfort level while I'm here. I'm certain my father won't be pleased to learn that I'm leaving town, but if I make it quick, I'm positive I won't miss anything crucial.

Honestly, I'm not entirely sure why I need to stay here anyway. I could just as easily fly out whenever they require my assistance. At least now I have an excuse to be working with my hands again.

My drive back from Denver was delayed, so I missed the scenic views. However, I'm glad I bought a truck. It's raining heavily now, and it's pitch black outside. I know there's a lot of wildlife behind the tree lines, waiting to dart out in front of me. Not today, Satan.

While I was downtown, between picking up the truck and shopping for appliances, I decided to stop for lunch and came across a local recreational dispensary.

When in Colorado, live like the Coloradan's, right?

I haven't smoked since college and thought it would be a nice way to unwind once I'm settled in.

I suffer from severe anxiety attacks every once in a while, particularly at night, and I'm hoping this may also be the answer when I'm at my worst. They get pretty scary and I've come close to passing out during one of my more severe attacks. I usually avoid taking medications whenever possible, and I'm already running low on my nighttime as-needed anti-anxiety medications. If this works for me, I might just let the next prescription expire and stop taking them altogether.

I'm feeling tired and still have an hour to drive, so I decide to resume an audiobook I had forgotten that I had started a few months ago. It's a dark romance about a man who stalks a woman every night outside her house. By chapter eight, I'm still not certain if she recognizes him or has even seen him, yet he's already fallen deeply in love, or lust, with her.

I have to have her I moan under my breath as I watch from behind the oak tree in her backyard. Silly girl, you should know not to leave your curtains open at night, I can see everything. I'll have to teach you a lesson about that another time, but for now I'll enjoy watching you touch yourself for me. My breath hitches and I feel a bead of sweat on my brow as I watch her intently. I have every intention on making her mine. I will chase her until her legs give out and she has no option but to capitulate to me. My little bird, soon you will be forever *chained to me, and you will get on your hands and knees willingly and beg for me and my cock to consume you.*

"Fuck!" I hit pause and take a deep breath.

Holy shit that's hot. Messed up, but hot.

I haven't gotten laid in far too long, and now my dick is just as hard as the antagonist's.

I'm not about to go stalking some random chick, but I will definitely need to take care of things when I get home. Now, I think I remember why I stopped listening to this.

I decide against resuming, and settle for listening to music the remainder of my drive. Half Life by Livingston fills my speakers as I slowly wind through the mountain, letting myself imagine this place becoming my new home. Maybe here I'll finally find a reason to break free from the business.

Chapter Six

RYLAN

I 've been settled into my new duplex for a few days now, and everything with the strip mall is progressing smoothly.

Between meetings, driving down to Denver for furniture and extra supplies, and managing the project at the job site, I haven't had much time to relax.

I haven't set foot back into Brews N Booze since that unfortunate misunderstanding. I take pride in being nothing like my father, and what that barista perceived about my initial visit in town clearly reflects Sterling Senior's personality, not mine. It's embarrassing and not at all how I want to be portrayed, especially since I'll be here for the majority of a year.

I contemplate stopping into the coffee shop on my way to work in the morning as I pull into my parking space in front of the duplex.

It's been a long day, but I was able to get off earlier than I have been due to the rainstorm that hit half an hour ago.

The allure of the shower is irresistible, as I'm covered in dirt from head to toe. My wrangler blue jeans and Carhartt boots are caked with grime, and my fingernails are filthy.

I can't help but laugh at the image of my brother or father getting their hands dirty for a contract. They'd never dream of doing manual labor, while I find it the most satisfying part of the job. To secure my stay here, I insisted on being a part of the crew, which is an unconventional request. I consider myself a jack of all trades and can't stand by and watch others do the work when I'm equally capable.

As I begin ascending the path leading to my duplex, I'm suddenly struck on the head. Curious about what might have fallen from the sky I look around just as I hear someone frantically shouting at me from behind.

"Oh my gosh! I am *so* sorry about that!" I turn around and immediately recognize the barista from the coffee shop.

She's got her hair down this time, and it's beautiful. It's a rich brown with a slight curl that falls down to her midriff. She's wearing a Paramore band t-shirt underneath an unzipped yellow raincoat with the hood up.

She's got the cutest dimples, thick rimmed glasses, her black leggings leave little to the imagination, and she's barefoot of all things.

I barely noticed her before, mainly because of the unfortunate conversation we had. But I'm noticing her and all her curves now.

She awkwardly juggles her keys, mail and phone with one hand, and a dog leash in the other.

"Oh! It's you. Uh.. sorry. It's hard to throw a ball with my hands full." She's beginning to look around me when suddenly she yells again.

"Watch out!" What is it this time I think as I feel something lunge up my back, is she out to get revenge on me for being an ass or something?

"This is Echo, sorry. She's deaf and not always the easiest to control. She loves people, don't know where she gets that from." She's nervous and clearly trying to remove herself from the situation.

"Oh hey pretty girl!" I say as I kneel down to pet the white fluff ball that is desperately trying to become one with me.

"Not a problem, I love dogs. Echo, huh? And she's deaf? Thats funny."

The dog gets a few pets and licks in before her owner makes her way towards us and clips her harness back onto her leash.

"I'm Rylan," I say reaching my hand out to shake her visibly full hands before stuffing it back into my jeans pocket.

"Bailey. Are you the one who moved into Jakes unit?" She says with her eyes glancing over to my duplex.

"Yeah, I couldn't spend another night in that motel and I'll be here for a while, so I thought it'd be best to make myself more comfortable."

Damn, how did I miss her eyes before now? They're the brightest blue I've ever seen in person. almost like they're photoshopped. I can't stop staring, and I think she senses it because just as I'm about to continue the conversation, she starts walking away and shouts out again.

"See ya around, Ryan."

"Ry-lan! It's Rylan." Not sure she heard me or even cared, the door was mostly shut before I finished correcting her.

This interaction was better than our first two, but I sense that I'll need to make a considerable effort to gain her attention. She doesn't exactly exude a people-person persona.

However, I can't seem to stop thinking about her captivating eyes. How did I fail to notice her at the coffee shop the first time, let alone the second?

She may not conform to conventional beauty standards, she wouldn't be a model or draw attention wherever she goes. Nevertheless, she possesses an undeniable allure to me. Those curves and those love handles. Fuck those love handles, I would love to grab a hold of them while I pump into her from behind and watch her ass clap against me as I thrust as deep as I can. And now my dick is hard. What the fuck, where is that coming from?

I really need to get laid, and that audiobook is not helping my situation.

Once inside my duplex I kick off my boots and head straight upstairs to my shower, not wanting to waste a single second, and get in there while the image of her in my bed is still fresh in my head.

One hand gripping my throbbing cock, and one hand bracing myself up against the shower wall, I begin to pump. Images of Bailey backing her ass up into me, biting her lip and letting out the smallest moan. I growl and give my balls a tug.

Fuck, this feels good. I can only imagine how good she would feel. I picture flipping her onto her back and bringing her knees up while I situate myself at her entrance. Her hair water falling off the edge of my bed, her back arching as I slowly slide into her. The pace of my strokes becoming much quicker and more needful now, I let out a final growl and shake as my release hits the shower wall. My knees are weak and if it weren't for my hand bracing me, I would've lost my balance.

It's been a few weeks since I've gotten off, and the amount of relief I feel is unmatched. But now I'm left with wanting more, the real thing.

Suddenly I feel myself relating to the stalker antagonist in the audiobook I've been listening to. Wondering if she's in her bed right now, sliding her fingers in and out of herself with my face in her mind. And just like that, I'm overcome with an overwhelming sense of guilt, my mind can be such a traitor to the rest of my body.

I don't usually objectify women like this, even in my mind. Hell, I'm not even one to watch porn.

Don't get me wrong, I'm no saint and I've been with my fair share of women, but I don't even know her, yet I'm thinking about her in ways that I probably shouldn't.

I quickly clean up and slide into a pair of boxers before dropping onto my bed feeling ten times more exhausted than I had prior.

Hopefully this release offers me the peace I need to get some solid rest tonight, and that I don't spend the evening wrestling with my morality or anxiety.

Chapter Seven

BAILEY

"I can't believe coffee guy, Ryan? Whatever his name is, lives here. Like, basically next-door to us here." I say to Aspen as she plops down with some popcorn on the couch next to me.

Her long black hair is up in a bun like usual, and she's wearing a set of pajamas with cats printed on them in typical Aspen fashion. She's gorgeous and vibrant and has this warmth about her that radiates to everyone around her. She's shorter than me at only 5'2", but she's feisty as hell and could take a grown man down if she needed to.

Every Thursday night, we have a tradition of watching a movie together to commemorate my first night living here.

I moved in on a Thursday, and we were so exhausted from moving me in all day that we crashed on the couch and watched Pretty Woman. That movie marked the true beginning of our friendship. Even when we're busy with work or other life commitments, and she spends most of her time with her boyfriend Micah, we always make time for each other on Thursday nights.

"Oooof, he is fine. The things I would do to that man, or let him do to me. Was he just as hot tonight?"

"Aspen! You have a boyfriend! And also, he was much dirtier this time."

Aspen wriggles her eyebrows at me and with a wink says, "Yeah he was!"

Okay, she's clearly not getting it. Why does she always seem to have sex on her mind?

Yes, he's 'fine' as Aspen put it, but is that all there is to him? I don't typically go for a man like him, and men like that don't typically go for a woman like me. Was there even really a point to continue thinking about him in any way? Probably not.

Sometimes I really despise the way my brain makes me feel about myself. I wasn't always this resentful towards my body or personality, these feelings didn't really start to creep up until Anthony cheated on me with Liz.

He told me it was because I wouldn't put out, and he assumed it was because I wasn't comfortable getting naked for him due to my weight. He wasn't completely wrong, but mostly it was because I was waiting for the right time.

I'm thankful I didn't waste my time or body on him and I understand how I'm better off without someone like that, but it still hurt more than I cared to admit to anyone.

"So-, are you gonna try to get to know this guy now that he lives next to us, or are you just going to pretend he doesn't exist, and that you're not blushing at the idea of seeing him again?" Aspen says with a nudge. I think she noticed I was drifting off into my thoughts.

"I don't know, what would I even say? There's really no point to even try, he mentioned being here for a while, but that also insinuates his residency isn't permanent," I swirl my glass of wine and take a sip.

"Of course Echo took an immediate liking to him, and he appeared to enjoy her company just as much. Maybe I'll ask him if he wants to have a play date with her. She could use more friends."

"You're joking. She's a dog, he's a man. You're acting so ridiculous. If you don't ask him to coffee next time you see him, I will. Micah would understand, this threat is for the greater good. No if's, and's, or but's."

She throws some popcorn over to Echo who is giving her the death glare and trying to mind meld to convince her to get up the goods, apparently it worked.

"Fine. Next time I see him, I'll attempt a genuine conversation and I won't do what I usually do and bail after the first few words are spoken. I'm not making any promises, but you can let Micah know I'm willing to try for the sake of your relationship. Cause I gotta be honest, he's one in a million and you need to keep him locked down."

Aspen throws her head back and lets out a roaring laugh, "Babe, I appreciate your sacrifice, but he's the one for me and we all know it. I don't think he'd actually let me leave him for another man at this point, and I'm honestly surprised he hasn't gotten down on one knee yet and locked me down!"

We spend the next hour and a half watching Marley & Me, sobbing through most of it of course and taking turns suffocating Echo with cuddles and kisses as if she was the dog in the movie.

I was so wrapped up in the emotional release, I completely forgot all about coffee guy, that is until I took Echo outside for her final potty break and came face to face with him again. Why the heck was he out here so late?

"Hey! Bailey, right? Caught you again so soon."

I was trying to avoid looking directly at him as my face and eyes were all red and puffy from all the crying I had just done. "Yep, heading to bed after this."

"Oh, gotcha! Same, I couldn't sleep and I left some sleep aids in my car that I thought I'd take, otherwise I won't be making it through tomorrow without an IV full of coffee and red bull." He laughs.

"Hey, are you okay?"

He steps closer to me and looks like he's going to bring his hand up to my chin but stops himself mid reach.

"Yeah, just had a therapy session in the form of a movie with a very naughty Labrador that becomes the perfect family dog just in time to die on them."

"Marley & Me, huh? Love Jennifer Aniston in that. I'm not too manly to admit I've cried to that movie a handful of times." He reaches down to pat Echo's head.

"Well, I'll let you get back inside then, if you're sure you're alright. Have a better night Bailey."

I watch as he gives a wave and walks to his front door that's on the end unit of our strip.

Ugh, I can't believe I ran into him again. Twice in one night, what are the odds?

I definitely won't be mentioning this to Aspen. For one, she's passed out on the couch and none the wiser, and for two I didn't come close to keeping up my end of the bargain.

It had been a week since I last ran into coffee guy. I was honest when I told Aspen I would give it my best shot at asking him for a coffee date, or something along those lines.

At the very least I would let the conversation go as long as he kept it going.

I may not be super confident in myself or my looks, but I can tell he wanted to talk longer each time I ran into him the other day, and I was the one being closed off and abrupt.

It's hard to believe this was the same guy, he seemed so friendly and outgoing now, it's almost unnerving.

I'm technically off work this morning, but I'm meeting with the shop's owner to discuss a few things.

Although I don't have an official title, I'm the closest thing Violet has to a shift lead. My responsibilities include filling orders and creating barista and bartender schedules.

Violet is not only the owner of Brews n Booze but also Micah, Aspen's boyfriend's, mother. Micah is the lead bartender here, and that's how they met.

On Aspens first shift as a bartender, she had a mishap and slipped, dropping a tray holding six glasses of Bud Light. Micah rushed to her aid, and from that moment on, they've been inseparable. While I'm not a believer in love at first sight, I genuinely believe in them and their relationship.

"Hey Bailey!" Violet says in a sing song voice as she walks up to the table I'm sitting at.

She's in her mid-fifties with her long blonde hair tied into a high ponytail, and wearing a pair of wranglers with a button down denim jacket over a black tank, and her favorite pair of Ariat boots. When she's not here, which isn't very often during the day shift, she's at her ranch working her horses.

She has the freedom to do all these things because her husband is Andy Pierce, Mayor of Elk Hollow.

"Hey Vy, how are things up at the ranch? Starlight healing alright from her accident barrel racing last month?"

"Oh you betcha! She'll be ready next season, guaranteed!"

"That's actually kind of why I called you up here this morning. I'm thinking about selling this place. I want to slow down and focus on Pierce Ranch. I was hoping you would help assist whoever comes in to take my place. I'll be sure to tell 'em that you staying on as a full time employee as second in command is part of the deal. If you're willing to stay on that is."

"Violet, I think that's a great idea! Have you thought about keeping it and putting Micah and Aspen in charge though? Micah practically runs the bar as is anyways, and I can help Aspen with whatever she needs to learn."

Violet shifts in her chair and places her hand up to her chin to tap it in thought.

"Now that's an idea! Let me think on it and I'll talk to the kids and get back to you. You're the best Bailey, thanks!"

With that she stands to give me a hug and heads back out to the parking lot.

Damn, I really hope Micah and Aspen agree to take over. That would be better than some rando coming in and taking over.

I do admire what Vy is doing though, and am slightly jealous of her ability to go for what she wants.

Chapter Eight

RYLAN

Seeing Bailey after she had been crying the other night, especially after imagining her in an questionable position with me beforehand, left me feeling a range of emotions I wasn't accustomed to experiencing. I yearned to reach out and touch her, providing her with a sense of security.

Once I understood that she was upset about a movie, I felt a sense of relief, but then I couldn't help but wonder what it would be like if her heart had been truly shattered over something of lesser significance.

I've never experienced what people refer to as a genuine relationship, characterized by commitment and love.

I've had casual encounters of course, especially in my younger years, some of which lasted for months. But there was never a deeper emotional connection beyond physical attraction.

The only women I've expressed my love for are my mother, sisters, and nieces. I believe I understand *how* to love a woman. The art and appreciation involved in it isn't lost on me. However, I've never met someone I felt I could spend the rest of my life with. I take the idea of commitment and marriage very seriously.

But seeing Bailey upset, now that feeling resembled the one I got when Tash had her heart broken before meeting Mikey. I wanted to hunt the guy down and knock him out for hurting her.

I don't know why I was feeling this way about a woman I don't know, but I do know that I intend on figuring that out as soon as possible. Otherwise I know I won't be able to focus on the reason I'm out here in the first place.

Speaking of the building plans, they are progressing exceptionally well. Once completed, the strip will house eight units. There are already potential plans for a sushi restaurant, a gym, a pub, and a flower shop.

Although my father may be a difficult person to be around, he has a knack for business, and a keen eye for when and where to invest. As a result, we have thousands of satisfied clients, and millions of dollars to demonstrate our successes.

It's lunchtime, and I didn't get much sleep last night, so instead of food, I opt for coffee.

Am I hoping to run into the alluring barista while I'm here? Of course I am. But I genuinely need caffeine, and what kind of person would I be to deny myself that pick-me-up?

I push open the doors and am immediately graced by the sight of Bailey behind the bar.

She's laughing hysterically at something the other barista must have said to her. Next thing I know, she's leaning over, laughing so hard that no sound comes out, while the other barista cackles and yells in amusement.

I genuinely wish I could understand what had triggered such a reaction from them, whatever it was must've been good.

"If you're laughing at me, I think that would earn me a free cup of coffee," I say with a straight face and stern voice.

Both girls immediately stop and stare at me silently. Shit, I wasn't serious, I guess I need to work on my delivery.

"I'm kidding! I guess I'm just a little jealous that I wasn't here to see what was so funny."

"Hmmm, you're cute, but not funny. That's a bummer." The other barista says before walking to the counter.

"Aspen, and you already know Bailey boo, my roommate and bestie for the restie."

Bailey boo? Bestie for the restie? Well, that's adorable.

"Ryan, right?"

"Oh," I chuckle. "No, it's Rylan. That's okay though. It's not a very common name and is often misheard the first time."

I can see Bailey's cheeks redden from what I assume is embarrassment. It's cute when she blushes.

"Bailey... Boo. of course I remember you. I hope your heart is healed from watching Marley & Me and all your tears have dried up."

"Ahhh!" Aspen shouts. "Why'd you have to bring up that damn dog? Now I'm going to be sad all day! I need to take a break and go watch Gilmore Girls or something. I'll be back."

With that she walks around the counter and into the back room. She was either serious, or she was secretly trying to give Bailey and I some space.

"She's very attached to Marley as you can see." Bailey says as she starts to pour fresh coffee into a to-go cup and hands it to me.

Her hair is in a high ponytail this time and it swishes back and forth as she walks.

An image of me wrapping one had around it and pulling her head back to look at me while I'm fucking her from behind flashes through my head and once again my cock is alive and well. Seriously dude, calm down.

"Clearly. Be sure to apologize to her for me."

"Yeah, I'll do that. Anyways-"

I can tell she's wanting to shut the conversation down as she takes a step back and points towards the back room.

"It was nice seeing you again, Rylan. I should probably get back to work though and make sure Aspen is recovered."

"Of course, thanks for the coffee."

I'm heading out the door when I realize how ridiculous I'm being. I'm a grown ass man, and I can't talk to a woman without getting flustered or second guessing myself? Before I know it, I'm turning around and stalking my way back to the bar.

"Bailey? Would you like to have dinner with me tonight?"

I can see her face turn pale, glancing back and forth between me and the door to the back room where a squeal is released.

"She'd love to! Pick her up at seven and keep her out until a minimum of one a.m, thanks!" Aspen yells, I can see her face behind the little window in the saloon door.

"Uhh. What she said? I guess." Bailey says while looking down at her feet and biting her lip. Shit she needs to not do that tonight if she wants me to be a gentleman.

I pull out my a business card from my wallet that includes my cell phone number and hand it to her.

"Perfect. Dress however you feel comfortable, no pressure."

Feeling confident and much more awake now, I head back to the job site.

I know I want to make tonight special, so I plan to get off early and run to the local market for some supplies.

I just hope she doesn't do too much internet stalking on me leading up to tonight.

I'm not quite prepared to delve deep into the Sterling business or family dynamic.

Chapter Nine

BAILEY

Being invited to dinner with Rylan was not on my 2023 bingo card, or any year bingo card for that matter.

I'm not sure I would've said yes if it hadn't had been for Aspen answering on my behalf. I love her, but girlfriend has zero chill.

I'm completely clueless about what to wear, and this is making me even more stressed.

He had advised me to dress comfortably, but what if I opt for leggings and a t-shirt, only to find him wearing a suit? That would be mortifying, although I can assume a suit wouldn't be his first choice, considering the only place to eat out is the diner, which isn't exactly a black-tie kind of establishment.

After trying on a few outfits, I finally decided on a pair of black leggings, blue Hey Dude shoes, and a long-sleeved babydoll shirt in black with white lace trim on the bottom and around the neckline.

The neckline falls quite low, but the lace covers my bra, providing *some* modesty.

The waistband cinches and is slightly slimming, effectively concealing my small but noticeable apron belly.

Aspen approves my outfit choice and gives me a hug as she heads off for her date night with Micah, leaving me to panic and overthink things alone.

It's already six, and I have an hour to get ready. I don't usually do much to my hair or face, but I want to look nice, so I curl my hair and put on eyeliner, mascara, and blue eyeshadow.

I tie the look in with blue studded earrings and a blue beaded bracelet from the farmers market.

This is as good as it's going to get tonight, and I hope he thinks I look alright. He must be somewhat attracted to me if he asked me out on a date?

The longer I sit and question his motives, the more anxious I become.

Should I text him and let him know that something unexpected has come up?

Just as I'm about to head to the kitchen for a glass of water and my phone, there's a knock at the door, and my heart drops to my ass.

I glance over at the microwave and it reads 6:58, *damn he's prompt*. No turning back now.

I open the door to see the most beautiful man standing in front of me with a bouquet of sunflowers, my favorite. How the hell did he know?

He's wearing blue jeans and a black button-up dress shirt with the top two buttons undone giving a peak at this bare chiseled chest, and his sleeves rolled up.

And *oh my God*, he has a sleeve of tattoos on his right arm that starts at his wrist, and extends up to where his dress shirt is rolled up just below his elbow.

I never would have expected him to have tattoos, but I'm not complaining and I'm eager to see if he has anymore hidden under there.

He flashes the most jaw dropping smile I have ever seen, and suddenly I feel a heat between my thighs and my breath catches and I almost choke.

The fuck? I am actually starting to choke, what the hell am I choking on?

I'm immediately hit with a feeling of panic, I can't breathe and I'm going to keel over at this ridiculously attractive mans feet.

My obituary would read "Death by simply forgetting how to breathe correctly." How embarrassing would that be?

I'm coughing but still feel a tightness in my throat that tickles and burns. I'm pretty sure my eyes are going to pop out of their sockets.

"Shit, Bailey! Are you okay?"

Between coughs and the few breaths I can take I manage to spit out the words "Yep. Choking. On. Air."

While I give him a not so conniving thumbs up.

Oh my God, I want to put a paper bag over my head and never show my face again!

He hastily steps around me to grab the glass of water left on my counter and hands it to me.

"Here. Drink this. Now." He says in a deep commanding growl.

Oh no, stop thinking about his voice and the animalistic sound that just seeped past his lips.

Drink the water, Bailey, focus on your breathing.

Ahh, sweet relief. But now I'm flustered for more than one reason.

"Thanks. That was a close one. You almost killed me and ended up on one of the podcasts I listen to." I say while blotting under my eyes with my finger trying to clean up the eyeliner that I'm sure is messed up.

"Let me just run to the bathroom real fast and I'll be ready to go."

He chuckles and nods his head as I head out of the kitchen.

Once I'm sure my makeup is fixed and I won't be having another coughing fit, we step outside and lock up.

He starts walking towards his unit when I remember he was holding something before I almost passed out.

"You brought me flowers, didn't you? I should run back in and put them in some water."

"Already did that. I used your drinking glass, hope that's alright." He stops and turns around to face me when we're halfway up the path to his place.

"Are you trying to bail on me Bail-y?"

"Ha, funny. No, I genuinely wanted to make sure the sunflowers were put in some water. Those are my favorite flowers and I didn't want them to wilt."

I was only half lying, they are my favorite flowers, but why is he bringing me to his house? Here I go, starting to overthink things again.

"Good. I set up something really special for you that I think you'll enjoy." He replies almost as if he could hear my thoughts.

He guides me through his front door with one hand on my lower back. As soon as I step inside, I'm greeted by the warm glow of candles illuminating the dining table, and an enticing aroma wafts from the kitchen, tantalizing my senses.

"Mmmm, what is that smell? You cooked?"

"Of course I did, I wasn't going to feed you diner food on our first date."

I giggle and gawk at the sight. No one has ever set something up like this for me before and it feels unreal.

"Blackened chicken with crispy parmesan potatoes, roasted garlic butter asparagus, and Pinot Noir to wash it down. I hope this is okay?"

I'm standing here blinking, at least I think I'm blinking, in disbelief. Taking it all in.

"Okay?" I whisper. "This is more than okay. No one has ever gone to this much trouble for me before. Thank you."

I start to choke up again, thankfully this time I can manage it without flailing around like a fish out of water.

I know he noticed my mood shift and voice crack because he begins to make his way towards me with a concerned look on his face, and a glass of water in his hand for me just in case.

"Here, let's sit down and eat, I don't want the food to get cold." He reaches around me to pull out my chair, again, something I'm not used to.

I've observed my dad with my mom, Alec with Becca, and Micah with Aspen. I understand this is how they interact, so I understand this is normal. However, it's not my usual experience.

Throughout the dinner, I've noticed a decrease in my body tension. I'm having an exceptionally enjoyable time, surpassing my expectations.

Moreover, I'm not overly concerned about the amount of food I'm consuming in front of him, which is also a new feeling.

"This is really delicious," I say in between bites. "When did you learn to cook like this?"

"Thank you, I'm glad you're enjoying it. When I was in college I took some classes with a private chef with a buddy of mine from my frat. That buddy went on to continue to train with him and is now a 5 star Michelin chef."

"Wow, that's incredible! I don't think I've ever dined at a 5 star Michelin restaurant."

His eyebrow raises like he's shocked and now I feel overwhelmingly uncultured.

"Maybe someday I'll take you to one. But if I'm being fully transparent, it's a lot of money for not a lot of food. Kinda overhyped if you ask me." He laughs, picking up our plates and walking into the kitchen.

After dinner, he suggests we have a cup of coffee or tea together before ending the date, I opt for the premixed Chai he has in his fridge. Not as good as the chai we have at Brews N Booze, but it's better than drinking coffee this late. Plus, I'm not a huge fan of it overall.

While I'm slightly disappointed that the evening is drawing to a close, I also feel a sense of relief because I'm beginning to experience feelings while sitting so close to him on the couch that we recently moved to. It's leather and with my soft leggings, I keep sliding closer to him and I have to subtly move my ass back onto my side of the cushion before our legs can touch.

He vaguely explained his reason for being in town, briefly mentioned his family and business, and inquired about my personal life.

Our conversation flowed effortlessly, but I sensed that we were both hesitant to delve too deeply.

It was as if we were afraid of saying the wrong thing, and driving each other away.

After finishing our drinks, he kindly offered to walk me home, even though it was only a few doors down.

"I had a great time tonight, beautiful. Thanks for coming over, I hope you'll agree to do this again with me soon." He says as we stand in my open doorway.

"Um, sure. Maybe. Thank you for tonight." I say with my head looking down at our feet.

Suddenly I feel his hand pulling my chin up to look him in the eyes. "Why do I get the feeling you don't mean that?"

"I guess I just don't understand. Why me? I'm not like the other girls that I'm sure you're used to going out with. I'm not a size three, and I have more flaws than I do perfections." I bite my lip, wondering if I shouldn't have said all that.

I know confidence is sexy and I am exuding the exact opposite of that right now. Smooth, Bailey.

"You're right," He says in a low growl. His eyes directed down at my lips.

"You're not like every other girl I've been out with, you're much more captivating and real."

Next thing I know, his lips are on mine, and my stomach is fluttering.

It's a soft kiss, with one hand still under my chin, holding me gently in place. I want to melt into his arms right here on this porch, and pop my foot out like Mia Thermopolis from The Princess Diaries.

"I hope it was okay that I kissed you," He says gently, pulling away from my lips with his hands still firmly in place.

"Uh. Yeah. Great? Good... kiss. Good... job?" What the fuck is wrong with me? His lips made me incompetent?

Rylan chuckles, "Did I break you?"

"Ha, uh, well... Goodnight." I say, walking backwards through the door, tripping over the frame on my way in. He reaches out to try to steady me.

"Goodnight," He says, stifling a laugh.

Once the door is shut behind me, I sink to the floor and place my hands over my face.

Oh my god that was embarrassing, and I would be incredibly surprised if I ever heard from him again.

Chapter Ten

RYLAN

It took everything in me not to back Bailey up into her apartment and take her right there in the entryway last night.

That kiss was mind-blowing. Like nothing I'd ever experienced before, and I wanted to keep exploring.

It didn't stem from lust or need, but from passion and something deeper.

I could tell she felt something, too. When I pulled away and told her goodnight, she looked like I had taken the breath right out of her.

And then the way she stumbled on her words... and feet. It was adorable as hell and I felt like a teenager with his first crush all over again.

I hated walking away, but I know she deserves more than a quick fuck. I need to show her that I'm not just wanting a one night stand.

Shit, I don't know what I want, or what I should want. I do know it's not that, though. I've had enough of that in my life, and none of it has ever felt like this.

No, this date was different. Especially with her choking on seemingly nothing incident, but that is something I'm assuming is right on par with her character in general, and I find it equally alarming and adorable.

I have a feeling I'll be spending a lot of time trying to protect her from herself.

It's a rainy Saturday, and unfortunately, there's no work for me to do at the site today. My anxiety attacks tend to be more frequent when I'm less active, so I decided to head to the school gym early this morning to burn off some energy and clear my mind.

Throughout the morning, I couldn't help but check my phone for a text from Bailey.

Feeling giddy and hopeful even though I know deep down that she's not the type to let her guard down and reach out first, especially considering her handful of insecurities.

What's the rule for sending a text after the first date? Is there still texting etiquette, or is that obsolete now that technology is so prominent?

"Hey Siri, what is the acceptable timeframe to text someone after a first date?"

Man, this is ridiculous, I've never thought this much about sending a damn text before.

It is generally acceptable to text someone the day after your first date to express that you have had a good time, and to gauge their interest.

Alright, that's an answer I'll accept. Now, I just need to formulate the message.

Hey, I've been thinking about you. Delete.

Hello, how are you doing today? Delete.

Hi Bailey, I had a great time last night. Want to do it again? Delete.

Fuck, okay. Maybe a combination of these.

> Hey! Hope you're having a good day so far, I had fun last night. :)

I hit send before I could contemplate any further.

I haven't looked outside to see if her car is here, and I don't want to be a creep so I refrain from doing so. For all I know she's been busy at work and I'm over thinking things.

Knock knock

Hmm, that's strange. Could she be skipping past texting me back and coming over to see me instead? It's highly unlikely, but I'm hopeful.

As I open the door, I'm practically knocked to the ground. Arms flung around my neck, and legs wrapped around my waist.

"Ry Ry!"

It's my baby sister, Natasha. When I moved in, I gave her my address and told her that if she was planning to visit the area, she should drop by and see me. I figured she'd let me know before she came, but she's a bit of a wallflower and goes with the flow, so I suppose she probably didn't even have a plan until the last minute herself.

"Tash? I've missed you!" I let her down and take a good look at her, she's growing up so fast and I can't believe how mature she looks now, not so much my baby sister anymore.

She's got dirty blond hair with green eyes, proba-bly weighs not much more than 100 pounds soaking wet at 5'1", and is wearing a drug rug hoodie and some hippy pants that look homemade.

"Did you just get here? Where's Mikey and the animals? Get in here, it's wet and cold," I say, glancing over her to see if I can spot him or the van.

"Mikey wanted to find a good place to park, and take Milo for a walk so I could have some chill time with my big bro!" She says punching my arm. "I've missed you so much, it's been what... four years?"

Shit, I didn't realize it had been that long since I've seen her, no wonder she looks so much more grown up. She was still just a teenager when I last saw her.

"You know you all can crash here, Tash. I have a guest bedroom, pets are allowed, and you can park in the lot off to the side."

I'm still standing in the kitchen when she walks over to the living room and slumps down onto the leather sectional and sprawls out.

"Ahhh, a full sized couch! Feels so nice. You've got a real great place here, Ry!" She sits up and turns to look at me with her arm draped over the back of the couch, and her chin resting in the crook of her arm.

"But you know, home for me is the van and I'd feel out of place staying here. Thanks though!"

"Well, how long are you planning on staying here, and what brings you by? Not that I'm complaining."

She gets up and walks over to the bar chairs in my kitchen to sit at the high counter next to where I'm standing. Her smile says happy, but her body language and eyes say otherwise.

"What's going on Tash?"

She starts half turning the swivel bar stool back and forth with her foot against the wall under the counter, and her hands gripping the edge of the bar. I can tell something is up.

"Mom and dad cut me off... and we've run out of money," She sighs.

"Milo needed emergency surgery a few months ago, and the van broke down a week later. It cost thousands of dollars individually for both emergencies. And then the cost of living just kept steam rolling us and we couldn't catch up."

She stops swinging the chair and looks up at me with puppy dog eyes.

"I promise that's not why I'm here. They cut me off two years ago, something about needing to go back to school. We've been fine because I saved up over the years, but our vlog and social media accounts aren't bringing in enough money to cover what happened, I also quit my art."

"How much do you need?" I say with a stern tone. I love her, and I understand she didn't do this on purpose. Despite her carefree ways, she's smart.

"I've maxed out every credit card-" She begins spinning again.

"Natasha... How. Much?" I growl.

"Thirty Five. Thousand?" She says just above a whisper.

"Fuck, Tash!" I didn't mean to sound so harsh but damn. My hands rubbing across my mouth and beard as I let out a sigh.

"Sorry, that came out more aggressive than I meant for it to. Will that dig you out of debt and give you a substantial cushioning, or just cover the credit cards? I need to know how much you need to get you back above water."

"Ry, I can't ask you to do this for me. I'm not your responsibility, and I feel awful bringing it up. I'm so sorry."

Stepping in front of her, I place my hands on her shoulders to comfort her and let her see that I'm not mad or disappointed.

"You are my sister and I will do anything for you. My finances are stable and I can afford to help. I love you, and I want to do this for you. Now please, give me a number. I'll write you a check, and then we can go get some food at the diner and catch up. Okay?"

She gives me a look of relief, her shoulders drop and become much more relaxed and she starts to tear up.

I meant what I said, I would do anything for her. I know our brother and sister would've turned her down and told her to figure it out for herself, but I could never do that. I can afford to help, so why wouldn't I? I know she would help me if I ever asked for anything. I don't think I could reach out to Rachel for personal advice, but I'm positive Natasha would know what to say if I ever needed any.

I write the check for fifty thousand, grab my coat and an umbrella, and together we walk out to my truck.

She called Mikey and he's going to meet us at the diner for lunch so we can catch up and talk about what their plan will be going forward.

I can't cover their finances for the rest of their lives, but I'm sure we can come up with a way for them to bring in real revenue and continue to be on the road, living life the way that brings them peace and happiness.

Chapter Eleven

BAILEY

Even though it was my day off, I had to go into the shop for a few hours this morning to write the schedules and place the order that's to be delivered next week.

Violet hasn't gotten back to me yet about her plans for Brews N Booze, and Aspen nor Micah mentioned anything about taking over so it's business as usual for now.

I don't like change very much, so I feel alright about that.

I'm finding myself thinking about the date with Rylan a lot today. I'm happy that I didn't overindulge in the wine with dinner, or stay out excessively late, but a part of me wishes he had come in after walking me to my place.

I'm still embarrassed about how I had acted after our kiss, but surprisingly, he sent me a text message about half an hour ago. I was about to leave the shop, so I decided to respond once I got home.

As I pull into the parking space in front of my unit, I spot Rylan stepping out from his apartment with an umbrella. Beneath it, a petite blonde woman.

She exudes beauty and radiates a sense of tranquility. Both of them are smiling and laughing, and my heart sinks, causing a wave of nausea to hit me.

Now that I'm fully parked, I try to stay as still as possible, hoping to avoid catching their attention. There are no cars parked in between us, just three empty spaces so I sink down as far as I can go while his back is facing my direction. He helps her into the passenger seat of his truck before walking around to his side and closes the umbrella before hopping in himself.

I didn't recognize her, so I know she's not from around here. Is she his girlfriend or just a booty call from back home? Did she fly out here to surprise him, or did he ask her to come?

I can't believe he spent last night making me feel special, only to send me a text while he has another girl in his house. I knew that was the type of woman he usually went for, so I can't help but wonder if he realized he has no business being with someone who looks like me. Maybe he's regretting it, or maybe it was a joke or a bet from someone he works with.

I wait a few minutes after they drive off the property before getting out of my car and heading inside. I didn't want to risk him being close enough to see me from the rearview mirror and know that I saw them.

I have no idea what I'm going to do about what I just saw. All I know is that this hurts like hell, and I knew I shouldn't have put myself in this position with a guy again. I barely know him, but he made me feel seen. Now I just want to be invisible.

Once inside, I swiftly pass by a sleeping Echo, and Aspen who is sitting on the couch watching some reality TV. She was so invested in whatever was happening with the Kardashians that she didn't even notice me coming in.

Aspen was thrilled to chat about last night, but now I have nothing positive to contribute to the conversation with feeling the way that I do. It pretty much negates everything good abut the date.

I'm hesitant to risk her noticing my distress, so I head straight for my bathroom and lock the door.

Knowing my penchant for extended reading sessions in the tub, she wouldn't suspect anything if I stay in here for a few hours.

As I close the bathroom door behind me, my phone vibrates, and I see it's a text from Aspen.

> Bailey! Where did you go?! I need all the juicy deets **immediately**!

> Hey girl. I have a headache, taking a bath. Catch up later?

> Aww, noooo! I'm sorry!! I'm heading to Micah's in an hour. Need anything before I go?

> Take Echo out before you leave please and thank you? Have fun, love ya!

> Of course! Love ya, too girlypop. See ya Monday!

I decide taking a bath and immersing myself in a book is actually a really good idea.

I don't want to be tempted to text him while I'm feeling like this, so I place my phone next to my bed on the charger and gather everything I need to take in with me.

By the time I come out of the bathroom it's close to 6 pm, and I'm properly pruned like a 90 year old and emotionally and mentally exhausted. At least I smell nice and my skin is super soft from the bath bomb that I had used.

I know I shouldn't, but I can't resist checking my phone once I step out. There aren't any new texts from Rylan which I admit is a little disappointing, though I don't understand why I was expecting anything different. He was still with the other girl for all I know, and despite my self-deprecating remarks, I recognize that I deserve someone to treat me me the way that Micah treats Aspen, and Alec treats Becca.

I open the door to let Echo into my room, wrap myself in my cozy blankets, and turn on one of my comforting go-to feel good movies, Big Daddy. With the tv muted, I also turn on the box fan on high to help me get a good night's sleep. The smartest thing for me to do right now is call it an early night, tomorrow will be better.

Chapter Twelve

RYLAN

When I got home from the diner yesterday it was pretty late in the afternoon, and I noticed Bailey's car was parked out front. I hadn't heard back from her yet, but I wanted to give her the time and space to wind down if she had a long day.

Lunch with Tasha and Mikey went well, and we came up with a solid plan to get them into a better situation.

They're heading to Dallas in a few days and will be staying at my condo. Since I won't be using it, there's no point in letting it sit empty when they could benefit from it.

Additionally, I've asked Carlos, my mechanic, to take care of the van to ensure its safety and reliability when they're ready to travel again. I don't want them worrying about running into issues with it again anytime soon.

They'll be able to use my car in the meantime so they can run errands outside of walking distance. They are so used to being on the open road and having endless freedom, so having my car at their disposal might help them feel a little less cooped up.

Natasha is going to promote their channel and resume creating and selling custom portraits. She'll have more time and energy to keep it going at my place than she did on the road. I also connected with a friend who owns a smoothie shop within walking distance of my house, and he offered Mikey a job for as long as he wants it.

These aren't permanent solutions if they plan on hitting the road again, but I'm hoping this will give them the time to form a bigger following, save money, and let Tash get back into the headspace she requires for her business.

With everything sorted, I sent Bailey a text this morning to check in and see if she was okay, but I hadn't received a response yet.

A few hours later when I went out to my truck, I saw her outside with Echo. As soon as our eyes met, she dashed inside. I'm clueless about what happened, but I'm not amused. I decide to confront her face-to-face and ask what's going on. The other night, we spent the better part of five hours together, and I had the feeling that we had a connection and chemistry. I don't understand why she's ignoring me now.

Bang *Bang* *Bang*

I wasn't in the mood to knock politely, and I wanted to make sure she heard me at the door. She can't claim she didn't know I was there if I knock loud enough.

It took about a minute for her to open the door for me. Before I could even open my mouth to speak, it seemed like she was about to shut it in my face. So, I quickly put my hand on the door to prevent it from closing.

"Why are you avoiding me, Bailey?"

Taking a step back, she gives me the silent invitation to step through the threshold now. She doesn't appear to be afraid of me, but she does seem upset and uncomfortable with my presence overall.

"Why do you even care, Rylan?" She barks back.

"Why do I care? Because I thought we had a nice time the other night?" I take another step towards her, she takes another step back.

"Do you not agree?"

"I thought we did, too. But apparently I was wrong. You can leave now, I'm sure your girlfriend wouldn't like it if you were spending time with another woman." This time she steps closer, trying to inch me back towards the door.

"Girlfriend? What the fuck are you talking about? I don't have a girlfriend."

"Rylan don't lie to me, I saw you two. Now please... Just. GO."

What the hell is she talking about? Why does she think I have a girlfriend? Saw us? Shit, is she talking about Natasha?

"Bailey. Stop." I growl. "You saw me with my sister. Not a girlfriend."

"Yeah. I'm sure that's who that was. Your sister." She says with a sarcastic tone.

"Jesus Bailey, will you listen to me? My sister Natasha and her boyfriend Mikey stopped by because they needed my help. They'll be staying at my condo back in Dallas for a while. Why the hell would I lie about this? Want me to have her come over and confirm, or can you just accept that I'm telling you the truth?"

She's standing in front of me with her arms crossed in front of her chest, rolling her eyes she lets out a huff.

"Sure, whatever, Rylan. I get it, okay? I'm not good enough for you."

"Stop being such a fucking martyr."

All she can do is stand there in silence, blinking at me like I had just slapped her across the face. I can't tell if she believes me or not, but honestly I'm too irritated to care.

"Look. You either believe me, or you don't. It's your choice. Stop deflecting your bullshit insecurities onto me though."

I turn to walk out the door when she grabs my arm and whips me around.

"I'm sorry." She whispers. I can see her eyes starting to water and her cheeks flush. Damnit.

"I'm just- I'm not used to being chosen. My ex left me for our coworker who I *thought* was my friend. They were hooking up behind my back and I guess-" Her voice cracks. "I guess I'm still broken from that situation. They really fucked with my head."

I can sense the pain in her voice, and the guilt that's rising is difficult to overlook. From an outsider's perspective, seeing my sister and me together yesterday might have raised suspicions. How was Bailey supposed to know that she is family?

"I'm sorry, too." I take a step towards her again, this time with a much less threatening vibe.

"You didn't deserve it, I hope you recognize that. And I wouldn't do that to you."

I gently reach down to her chin, tilting her face up to meet my gaze with one hand. My other hand cradles her face with my palm, while my thumb gently wipes away a tear from her cheek.

She's hurting, and I made it worse like such a dick. I don't even understand why I lashed out at her so quickly. I think I'm just used to being involved with a certain type of person, and she's nothing like that. She's much more fragile and insecure. Lashing out and throwing blame and insults at her isn't the way to handle things. That's something Sterling Sr. would do, not me.

"What I said was cruel. If anything, I was the one deflecting, and I'm really sorry."

"It's fine." She's pulling away now, and all I want to do is pull her into me.

"Please, let me fix this. I can't take back what I said, and I can't change what they did, but I can prove to you that you're worth more than you think you are."

"I'm sorry for assuming the worst." She says.

I decide to act on my urges and pull her into my embrace. I kiss the top of her head, her hair smells like a blend of vanilla and strawberries and it's intoxicating. Just like the sensation of her in my arms.

We stand there, holding each other for a few moments. When she pulls away, she looks up at my lips, inviting me in to kiss her. I know I shouldn't, not after everything we've been through tonight, but I need to be closer to her.

I lean down and press my lips against hers. They're soft and full, and I can taste the strawberry chapstick she must've applied before answering the door for me. It starts off sweet and innocent, but before I can stop myself my tongue is pushing past her lips and thrashing around hers. One hand reaches the back of her head and starts to gently tug on her hair, while the other is now moving up from her hip and beginning to explore more of her body over her baggy sweatshirt.

At some point I ended up walking her backwards and pinning her up against the wall, pressing my body into hers. She lets out a little moan and I just about lose it.

"Fuck, Bailey." I breathlessly let out in between kissing her.

She has one hand on the side of my ribcage, while the other hand has moved to the front. She lifts my shirt as her fingers tease the waistband of my jeans. I'm hard as fuck and my erection twitches every time her fingers get closer to being inside my boxers.

I slide my hand up her sweatshirt and she flinches, and not in a positive way but in a defensive, embarrassed way.

"It's okay." I softly attempt to reassure her.

My hand begins to travel further, a little at a time trying to ease her into my touch on her bare skin. She feels so good. But she winces and tries to pull away when my hand caresses her stomach. I can feel her rolls and tummy. No, she's not flat, but it's not a surprise to me and I'm definitely not complaining. However she is uncomfortable in her body and I need to be respectful but also show her what she's doing to me.

I remove my hand from under her shirt, and grab hers that has been teasing the front of my boxers. She needs to feel me, she needs to feel the reaction my body has to hers. I slide her hand a little further down over my jeans, and place it onto my cock. I guide her fingers around the bulge and hold it there. With a slight squeeze, her eyes widen and she shudders a breath.

"This is how my body is reacting to touching you, exploring you. My cock is enjoying every. Single. Inch. Of your body. Every. Single. Pound. Of your body."

With one hand braced up against the wall behind her, the other now on the side of her head wrapped into her hair, I place my face in the crook of her neck and kiss her softly. She moves her hand back onto my hip as I begin to lightly thrust forward in a circular motion into her. She moans and pulls her knee up into my groin while gripping my hair with her other hand.

"We-we need to stop." She squeaks out between breaths. I pull away to look at her, trying to gauge what our next moves will be. Fuck it was hard to stop, my dick is painfully tight in these jeans.

"What's wrong? Did I do something?" I'm holding her hands in mine now with our fingers interlocked. She's not pulling away, but I can feel the moment is passing for her.

"No! You didn't do anything wrong, I think I just need to take it a little slower. Maybe have a little more time to mentally prepare for things going further. Is that alright?"

Well I'm not going to be the asshole that tells her I won't hurt her, and then tell her I can't hold out for sex. Fuck, I've got to do the right thing here and say goodnight. Sooner rather than later so I can get these pants off of me.

"Of course that's alright. We'll go as slow, or as fast, as you'd like to." I start walking to the door. "I'll let you get some rest. Text me later?"

She opens the door to see me out, and I turn to kiss her on the top of her head. "Goodnight, beautiful."

"Goodnight, Ry."

As I'm walking back to my place, I'm left with the taste of her on my lips, and realizing that she called me Ry; no one aside from my siblings and Callum has ever called me that. Fuck, this girl is something else.

Chapter Thirteen

BAILEY

I t's been a few weeks since Rylan and I had that moment of shared intimacy in my kitchen that I quickly shut down despite the feeling between my legs. He didn't appear to be upset with me for ending it, and he even sent me a reassuring message the next morning to ease my concerns.

Work has been quite interesting, to say the least. Vy had asked if I would like to take over for her so that she could focus on the ranch, and of course, I said yes. I love her and want her to do what brings her joy, even if it makes me feel a little uneasy and brings extra stress to my workload.

Micah agreed to take over the bar full-time, but Aspen isn't ready to take over the coffee shop at the moment. I don't necessarily want it either so I understand her trepidation, but I'm hoping it won't be too long before she is ready.

Yes, my dream is to eventually own my own coffee shop, but not this one. Fortunately, the position change came with a generous pay raise for both Aspen and me, as she assumed my former responsibilities.

I was able to hire a girl fresh out of high school to fill Aspen's shifts, and Micah hired another bartender, reducing the need for frequent role exchanges between bars and their employees. At this point, no one should have to cover both unless they choose to.

In my free time, I've spent more time with Sandy and Rob, our neighbors next door. I'm often invited over to their place for coffee and music on their back patio after dinner. We've also started a book club with a few others in town, which meet every Tuesday at Brews N Booze.

Since it's summer now, Rob and Sandy's kids and grandkids were able to stay with them last week, which was much-needed for everyone involved. They have the best family ever and I'm so thankful to feel like I've been made an honorary member of it.

Aspen has been working a lot more than she'd like, so I mostly see her at work, except for our weekly movie nights. She spends most of her free time with Micah, which is completely understandable. We're both extremely secure in our friendship, and we know that when one of us needs the other, they will be there no questions asked. She truly is the best friend I've ever had and could ever ask for.

I've been seeing Rylan whenever our schedules allow, which isn't often despite us living next door to each other. However, he's taken a few extra days off from work during the week to hang out with me. I know his family owns the company he works for, but we don't discuss it. All I know is that he works construction on the new building across town. I believe construction workers earn decent wages, but I'm aware of the high cost of rent here, so I can't help but wonder how he manages to afford taking time off.

He surprised me by requesting a long weekend, and I managed to rearrange my schedule and clear Friday through Monday this week. It's now Wednesday, and I'm clueless about what we're doing. He assured me that it would be worth it and that I shouldn't worry about Echo. Either that means we're staying here, or he's made arrangements with Aspen to watch her for me. She's the only person I trust with her, and he knows that.

> Should I pack for Friday?

Nope, that's not necessary. Don't stress it too much.

> If we go somewhere and I don't have a book, I'm going to be very intolerable.

LOL Fine, charge your e-reader if you must.

> You really aren't going to give me details, huh?

He's really not making this easy on me, and as much as I love surprises, I don't love being unprepared.

Nope. ;)

Rude.

You know you're excited.

It's Friday and my nerves are completely shot. I tossed and turned all night and my stomach is seriously pissed at me this morning.

Rylan texted me around 4 AM letting me know he was going to the gym and that he would be over around seven. I've been up since five, and am showered and mostly ready for whatever he has planned.

My e-reader is charged and in my oversized bag along with a few other items just in case. I know he told me I didn't need to pack, but I like being prepared.

Knock *Knock*

Of course, it's seven and he's here right on time. We are polar opposites in that regard, actually pretty much every regard. I'm late for everything, every time, without fail and it drives him crazy.

I open the door to find him holding a single sunflower with a hot-to-go cup in one hand, and another cup in the other.

"Mmmm, please tell me that's tea," I say practically bouncing at the prospect of my favorite drink being in one of those cups.

"Of course. Cinnamon Spice with honey, right?"

Grabbing the cup and holding it just under my nose to breathe in the delicious smell, I let out a sigh.

"Ahhh, yes. You're my hero."

"Wow, way to stroke my ego. Ready to go?"

"Yes. Thank you for the tea, and flower. Let me just put this in some water and we can head out to-" My voice trails off hoping he'll finish the sentence for me.

"Nope. Nice try." He laughs. "Hey, where's Echo's harness and leash? I'll get her ready."

I pause, facing him with a puzzled look. We're taking her wherever we're going? That's interesting.

If he expects me to hike in the deadass heat I'm not going to be happy.

He's wearing jeans and a black t-shirt that hugs him in *all* the right ways. His shoes don't appear to be anything made for hiking, so I think I'm safe. At least I better be. He's got to know by now that I'm not the adventuring outdoorsy type.

"Coat closet, in a basket up top." I say while filling a skinny bottle neck vase for the single sunflower.

"Does she need food or anything else?"

"Nope. I've got it all covered." He says while clipping on the harness. She is a very social dog in general, but she's really taken a liking to him. That's a good sign, right? Animals can sense when someone has pure intentions can't they?

Soon, we're in his truck descending the mountain. Echo is in the cab, accompanied by two suitcases, a duffle bag, and a box fan that I noticed. I've turned on my location for Aspen, just in case, but she assured me she was informed about the plans and played a crucial role in executing them. I have no reason to be concerned, and she knows I'll have a great time. At least one of us is confident.

He grants me complete access to the auxiliary chord, and I effortlessly switch between playing nineties pop, post-hardcore, and some of my favorite bands and artists, including Sleep Token, Post Malone, and Taylor Swift. I can discern his musical preferences, but he sings along to N'Sync just as enthusiastically as he does Falling in Reverse.

We're halfway to Denver when we pull over to let Echo out and grab some more tea and coffee. Despite the lack of direction or purpose, I'm content to savor the drive and the anticipation it brings.

Occasionally, he reaches over to gently place his hand on my leg, hinting at a desire to do more and linger longer. However, he resists the urge.

Ever since that night in my kitchen, he's maintained a respectful distance, allowing me to dictate the pace of our relationship. This dynamic stirs a mix of nerves and excitement within me, and I yearn to be fully prepared to give him more, perhaps even everything.

Rylan makes me feel things that I've never experienced before, and I can see myself caving to him sooner rather than later. I just hope that when I do, I won't regret it.

Chapter Fourteen

RYLAN

We've just arrived in Denver, and I can see Bailey's mind racing as she tries to figure out our destination now that we've gotten off the freeway.

Throughout most of the drive, she sat criss-crossed, with one foot folded under her and the other dangling off the seat, or with both feet up on the dash, while belting out lyrics to the most eclectic playlist that I've ever heard. Her personality truly shines when she lets her guard down. It's intoxicating, and it makes me want to do everything in my power to make her feel safe and happy as often as possible.

I pull up to a private airport where my company jet is waiting for us, and then onto the airstrip where the valet will come to retrieve my truck.

"You ready?" I ask as I throw it into park and glance over to gauge her feelings.

"Uhh.. ready for what? Are you secretly Christian Grey?"

I chuckle. "Who? Is that one of your book boyfriends?"

"Are we really getting on that?" She points towards the jet and then glances back at me wide eyed.

I can tell she's starting to feel more reserved again. I didn't even think of the possibility of her having an aversion to flying.

"It's a quick flight, and you'll have Echo as a security blanket," I say reassuringly.

She glances back to her sleeping pup. With a nod and soft smile she slips her shoes back on, and begins to gather her belongings that are spread out between the floor and console. I take that as her sign of approval to board.

"Good morning Mr. Sterling. Good to see you."

"Jeff Banks, good to see you. But, c'mon man, call me Rylan."

I nod towards Bailey and introduce her while Echo lets out a bark and tries to jump up onto Jeff.

"And this is Echo, our new mascot," I chuckle as I hold back the leash while I balance my duffel in the other hand.

"Of course, Rylan. And hello there ladies, welcome. I'll be your captain today. Once Trevor and Stacy are finished unloading the car we'll be on our way. Let us know if you need anything."

I let Bailey head up the stairs first and am thankful for that because in true Bailey fashion, she trips and almost stumbles backwards. I lightly push her forwards and she's able to stable herself with her hands on the step ahead of her. Her ass in a pair of tight black leggings juts out in front of me, and I can vaguely make out that she's wearing underwear with red hearts on them. Cute.

I stifle a laugh and bark out the word, "Careful."

She regains her balance and glances back at me.

"Oops!" She giggles.

Hell she's adorable. But I wonder if she's aware her leggings do not pass the squat test.

Once onboard, she selects a seat facing the front of the aircraft and attempts to fasten her seatbelt. I pretend not to notice her embarrassment when Stacy approaches to assist her in loosening the belt so it can be securely fastened around her.

Echo nonchalantly jumps up onto the seat next to her and curls up as if she's been here before. I slide into the seat directly across from them and buckle myself up.

"Are you excited?" I ask as she tucks a stray hair behind her ear and glances out the small window beside her seat, bouncing her knee up and down in a fidgety manner, I can't help but notice her restless energy.

"Very. But I wish I knew where we were going."

"You'll find out soon enough."

"Ok." She smiles cautiously.

"You're not just a construction worker or contractor. Are you?"

I give a half smile and a chuckle.

"No. No I am not."

The flight from Denver to Dallas, which is only two hours long, went exceptionally well. We spent most of the flight playing two truths and a lie, and we had a quick lunch in between.

I brought Bailey here to show her where I'm from and finally let her into my private world, which I've been hiding from her for the past few months. Tash and Mikey are visiting his parents in Corpus Christi for the weekend, and my house cleaner has been by to tidy up the place and pack their belongings into the guest bedroom while we're here.

I'm excited to show Bailey my favorite spots, but I'm also nervous that she's not going to like this side of me. For a brief moment, I debated introducing her to my family, but I'm worried about the judgement my father and brother will pass onto her especially.

She was right, she's nothing like the other girls I've dated or had been seen with by my family and friends. And not just in looks, but in personality as well. She's much more down to earth and kind. She's not superficial like everyone else is in my world.

She also doesn't come from the same background I was raised in, and my father has a tendency to look down on others that aren't aligned with his social status. My brother Kyle isn't *as* judgmental as the patriarch of the family thankfully, but I need to do this the right way if I'm going to do introduce them at all this trip or any other time.

Once we landed, a car was waiting to take us to my condo, which was only about a half-hour from the airport. She quickly figured out our location and expressed her excitement about being in Texas for the first time, despite the hot and humid weather.

Upon arriving at my condo and opening the door, her jaw dropped in surprise.

"I've never seen a place this nice before. Oh my god, the view!"

She drops her bag on the floor, kicks off her shoes and skips over to the large window in my living room that overlooks the city.

I'm in a penthouse and the views are incredible, I will admit. But nothing compared to the mountains I've grown accustomed to seeing every morning when I step out my front door back in Colorado.

"I'm glad you like it. I chose this place for the views."

The doorman steps inside with the rest of our bags and I slide him a tip as I close the door.

"Want to help me unpack and get Echo's stuff set up really quick?"

It's hard for her to pull away from the floor to ceiling window. Reluctantly she saunters over to the entryway and picks up her bag.

"I promise you can stare out the window for hours and watch the sunset later if you'd like to." I laugh as I pick up my suitcase and the box fan that I bought for her. Aspen is a saint and let me know that Bailey struggles sleeping without the white noise of a fan.

"Her bowls can go in the kitchen under the bar," I hand her a bag, "Here's yours and Echos stuff that I had Aspen pack for you."

"Thanks! Where's my room?" It's cute that she thinks we're sleeping in separate rooms.

With a crooked smile, I pick up my bags and lead her down the hall past the kitchen to my bedroom.

My master suite boasts a full-length panel window, just like the one in my living room. It also has a cozy fireplace, king-sized bed, and a spacious walk-in closet. Additionally, there's an attached master bathroom with a relaxing soaking tub, a full-sized sauna and steam shower, and a double vanity.

As she takes in the room, her eyes widen in amazement.

"I get to sleep in *here*?" If this is your guest bedroom, I can't even begin to imagine what the master looks like!"

Heading to the closet to unpack my bag, I casually mention that this is the master.

"Wait- are you taking the guest bedroom?"

"Nope," I say popping the P.

"My sister and her boyfriend's stuff is stashed in the guest room while they are out of town. This is the only available room in the condo right now."

She's still standing in the middle of the bedroom when I step out of the closet.

"Want help with your bags?" I ask knowing damn well she's freaking out internally.

"So, we're sharing a bed?"

It's adorable that she's pretending to be clueless.

I know I agreed to take things slow, and I won't force anything onto her that she won't want, but sharing a king sized bed doesn't mean anything has to happen.

"And the fan. You brought that for me? Won't that keep you up?"

"I'll sleep just fine. And the bed is big enough for us to have our own sides. Echo can even sleep in between us if you'd like."

That must have made her feel comfortable enough because she goes into the closet to unpack her bag as well, and shortly comes back out with Echo's bowls.

I don't expect anything to happen with her on this trip, but I would be lying if I said I wasn't hopeful that she might want to speed things up a little bit while we're here.

Chapter Fifteen

BAILEY

Once we were unpacked and Echo was fed, Rylan offered to take her down for a walk; giving me some much-needed time to myself and a chance to shower before dinner. After a long day of traveling, I was feeling filthy and was eager to get clean and comfortable.

As I made my way to the bedroom, I carefully scanned the walls and tabletops, hoping to find any pictures or other clues that might help me get a better idea of who this man is.

There is a single photo on the table by his front door next to a bowl that he tosses his keys and wallet into. It's a very formal looking family portrait with a man and woman in the middle, four adults, one of which being a slightly younger Rylan, a teenage girl that looks to be about seventeen, a toddler, and a newborn baby surrounding the pair. I recognize the teen as his sister Natasha that had visited him in Colorado a few weeks ago.

He appears to be very minimalistic, and his style is modern and very dungeon-esque. The bedding is all black, and I just know he will regret letting Echo sleep up there once her hair changes the color of his comforter from black to white.

There's a door separating the toilet from the main part of the bathroom, but not one separating the bathroom from his bedroom. It's all very fancy and screams high class, but also doesn't allow for much privacy, which makes me a tad nervous.

His shower is twice the size of mine back home, and there are dual shower heads and a bench on each side. It's like a freakin' his and her's shower and I've never seen anything like it!

On the other side of the bathroom there is a giant soaking tub that's calling my name and if I wasn't in a hurry, I absolutely would've chosen to take a bath instead of a shower.

The tile in the bathroom is heated, and there is a towel warmer he set up for me before leaving.

It's not cold in Dallas by any means, but having an open bathroom of this size probably doesn't allow for steam to generate outside of the enclosed shower walls, so I'm thinking I'll appreciate the added amenities when I step out with wet hair.

I turn on some music using the smart speaker on the bathroom counter, and just as I go to step into the shower I realize I forgot to grab clean clothes. His towels aren't meant for bigger people like me, and I have the choice between either letting my ass, or my lady bits and stomach hang out. I opt for the front and make my way to his walk in closet.

Sifting through my clothes, my back is turned to the entrance and I don't hear anything or anyone over the music and shower running. The towel slips from my hands while I reach up to pull my robe off the hanger, but thankfully my ass is big enough it catches it and doesn't fall completely to the ground.

"Fuuuck."

I snap around to see Rylan standing in the doorway of the closet, realizing that nothing is covered at this point and he is taking all of me in.

I hastily cover as much as I can with my robe.

"What the hell are you doing?" I shout at him, feeling *beyond* mortified.

"Shit, I'm sorry, Bailey. I heard the music and shower running. I thought you were in there, not in my closet!" He says gesturing to the bathroom.

"I really didn't do this on purpose," He runs his fingers through his hair and bites his lip. "But fuck, you're beautiful."

"Yeah right, Rylan." I bark back, turning around to quickly pull the robe on and tie it at my waist before facing him again.

He begins to step closer to me, "I mean it. Why can't you see yourself the way that I see you?"

My feelings of self doubt are crippling and getting in the way, that's why.

"Why would someone that looks like you be interested in someone that looks like me?"

I know how ridiculous I sound, I know I should believe him. Why would he bring me here and relentlessly pursue me if he wasn't attracted to me?

"Let me prove just how interested I am in you, Bailey. Trust me. Please."

Closing the space between us now, my heart is racing and my skin is tingling, begging to be touched by him.

Taylor Swift's Don't Blame Me is blaring in the bathroom and the shower still running.

He brings his hand up to my mouth, pulling at my bottom lip with his thumb before he continues to glide his hand down my face, to my neck, and then my shoulder where he stops. His hand then begins to slide the robe off of my shoulder slowly, exposing my left breast.

Biting his lip and sucking in a breath, I can feel his eyes scanning every part of me that he can see, and using his imagination for what he cannot.

"Goddamn, Bailey." I can see his erection growing underneath his grey sweatpants, and I want to reach down and wrap my hand around it.

"Can I keep going?" He asks as he tilts my chin up so he can look into my eyes. My body is screaming yes, but my head is saying no.

"Yes." I guess my body won this war.

"But- I need to tell you something first."

He stops caressing my arm and looks at me, giving me his undivided attention.

God I don't want to admit this to him, Aspen doesn't even know. I can't not tell him though, he needs to know what to expect with me.

"I'm a virgin. I've never done this before and I'm nervous."

I barely got the words out before a guttural sound escapes from his throat.

His eyes darken, and he's leaning down, forcing my lips to part with his thrusting tongue. His hands cupping my face, he pulls away and with a soft but demanding tone instructs me to climb into his bed.

I'm terrified but do as he says, pulling the blankets over myself, hiding as much as possible.

I believe I'm safe and am not necessarily afraid of him, but I am afraid to expose myself and give my all to someone. Especially this early on in a... whatever this is. We aren't even in a relationship and I'm bending to his will.

Am I seriously going to do this?

Of course I've messed around with guys, and I've been close to getting to this point before. But with Rylan it feels different. He does things to my body and soul that I have never experienced before and it's exhilarating.

I watch as he makes his way back into the bathroom, my mind and heart are racing and my body is vibrating and feels hot. I'm going back and forth on if this is the right thing to do. I really don't want to regret this, and I have no idea *how* to even do this. What if I'm horrible in bed?

All it takes for me to convince myself that I'm truly going to go through with this, is seeing him walk back into the bedroom towards me. He looks sexy and my body is desperate for him now.

Chapter Sixteen

RYLAN

I had a feeling Bailey was a little less experienced, and I knew she struggled with body dysmorphia and lacked self confidence, but her being a virgin is *not* what I was anticipating.

I guided her to the bed as calmly and gently as I could, commanding her to get under the covers and stay until I returned.

It took everything in me not to maul her right then and there. Knowing there has never been another man inside of her turned me on more than I could've imagined.

"I'll be right back, stay there," I say as I make my way to the bathroom to switch off the water that is still running. I leave the music on though assuming she might appreciate having it, and if I make too many abrupt changes in her surroundings, she may snap out of whatever this is that is allowing her to trust me.

"Will you feel more comfortable if we only have light from the fireplace?"

She bites her lip and nods, "Yes please."

Once the lights are off, it was just bright enough to make out her silhouette from the foot of the bed. This isn't what I would prefer, but tonight is about her, not me.

Kicking off my shoes I climb under the sheets with her. She's sitting up in the middle of the bed and appears to be frozen in place, not quite sure what to do with her body.

"Can you lie down on your side and face the window, please? You're okay, I promise." I say in a soft tone.

She does as I ask and lays down. Pulling her closer into me, I curl my body into the curve of hers and trail my fingers down her side, tempting my way to her warm center.

Her pulse began to quicken, and the goosebumps on her arm begin to form while she gently lifts her leg to let my fingers explore a little further.

"You're so fucking beautiful," I growl into her ear while peppering soft kisses up and down her back.

I take my time, becoming familiar with every inch of her. Tracing every curve and line of her body, taking note where her body reacts the most to my touch.

She backs into me with a slow but steady rhythm, rubbing up against my cock that is primed and ready for her.

"I want more," She whispers. "I want you."

That's all she needed to say before I was sliding my sweatpants and boxers down, reaching for a condom on the bedside table.

I want to watch her as I slide myself into her. I flip her onto her back and lower myself down to her, kissing her deep, our tongues thrashing together.

Her dormant sexuality is being awakened by my touch, her eyes have a fire lit inside of them as her fingers dig into my skin.

She's grasping, trying to satiate the desires now inside of her.

I slowly tease one, then two fingers inside, with the palm of my hand rubbing against her clit. She gasps and arches her back.

Sliding down to her center, I want to taste her, I want to feel her pulsing on my tongue. I spread her legs, wrap my hands around her thighs and hold onto her love handles as my tongue laps at her folds and sucks on her clit.

Her legs are quivering and it doesn't take her riding my mouth long before she's releasing her juices onto my tongue. Once she's finished and I've licked her clean, I make my way back up to her, kissing her as I tease my cock along her slit.

Bailey

The feeling of his length rubbing up against me, teasing me, is more than I can bare. I want, no need, to feel him inside of me. Bringing my knees up and wrapping my legs around his waist, he's situated himself in between them, with his arms bracing himself up, and his hands by my head.

"Kiss me," I say. I want to be closer to him, to taste him.

Propping himself up with his elbows and fore-arms now, his hands push the hair from my face as he leans in to kiss me passionately and fully.

Moving one arm between us and down to his cock, he begins to tease my opening, the head lightly pushing through my slit.

"Is this okay?" He shudders.

I moan and dig my fingernails into his back, "Yes. Keep going."

Slowly, he pushes himself into me, inching his way in little by little. He pushes and pulls, creating more slickness with each pass back and forth, making it easier for him to glide inside.

"Oh my God, Rylan!" I yell. Fuck it hurts but feels better than anything I've ever felt before.

"Goddamn, Bailey. You're soaked, and so tight."

Just as I think he's gone as deep as he could, he pumps again and I feel the base of his shaft hit the outside of my core, a light rub against my clit and I'm seeing stars. I wince and he pauses.

"Shit, are you hurt?" He asks concerned.

"Keep going."

Animalistic and needfully now, I can see his jaw muscles tighten in the dim light as he pushes and pulls, thrusting in and out of me.

"Fuck Bailey," He's panting, the veins in his fore-arms protruding and a bead of sweat on his brow.

"I'm going to come. You feel so good, come with me, baby."

A river of pleasure rushes through me, heat pooling to my core. I let out a cry, the release sending my body into convulsions. Riding this wave with me, Rylan leans back down, kissing me, stroking my hair as he continues to pump in and out of me, picking up the pace and force.

"Fuck, I'm coming," He growls.

His head falls next to mine, kissing my neck softly as he twitches inside of me, his rhythm slowing to a halt before he slides out of me and goes to stand.

He walks to the bathroom, and I hear the shower turn on again. He returns to the bed and calmly asks me to stand while he extends his hand for me to grasp.

"Let's shower. Once I'm out, I'll change the bedding."

Change the bedding? I stand and look down at the bed behind me, the light from the bathroom shines through just enough to see that I bled on the sheets.

It's not a horror scene by any means, but there is blood. I wince, "I'm sorry."

"Don't apologize, it's normal for some women to bleed their first time. Are you in any pain?"

"No, I don't think so." I had felt some light pain during, but the pleasure I felt was much more memorable and worth any discomfort I felt then, or now.

He helps me clean up and washes himself before getting out to run a bath.

After a few moments, I see him reappear behind the glass shower doors. He sets my e-reader, a glass of red wine, and a simple yet elegant charcuterie board on a small table next to the bathtub. Then, he pours what looks like bubble bath into the tub and places a fresh towel in the towel warmer. Opening the shower door, he reaches in to turn off the water and takes my hand to help me step out.

"Why don't you take a bath while I change the sheets? Feel free to stay in here as long as you'd like, but please don't fall asleep."

The music has been turned down and replaced with guitar covers of popular songs I've heard on the radio at work.

He helps me step inside the tub, and once I'm situated he bends down to kiss me. "Enjoy your bath, baby."

I feel like the prettiest woman in the world right now, despite the fact that I'm completely exposed.

Shortly after Rylan heads out of the bathroom, Echo enters the bedroom and rushes straight to me. She gives me a quick hello and lies down on the rug in front of the tub, curling up to sleep.

I had no idea what awaited me when I stepped out of the bathroom, but there he was, Rylan, sitting up in bed, engrossed in a book.

I cleared my throat, and he glanced up at me, a playful smile tugging at the corners of his lips. "Hey, beautiful lady, are you ready to catch some Z's?" he asked, adjusting his reading glasses and placing the book on his lap.

I nod in response, and he sets his belongings aside on the table next to him. Then, he stands to turn the fireplace off and the box fan on.

Sliding back into bed, he lifts the blankets for me to crawl in next to him. I turn on my side, facing the window as he pulls himself up against me, pressing his center into my back while bringing his arm under mine. With his hand resting under my breasts, he gives me a tight squeeze, kisses my neck, and says goodnight.

A wave of exhaustion overcomes me. Within minutes I'm drifting off to sleep with the warmth of Rylans body against mine and an unfamiliar feeling of security.

Chapter Seventeen

RYLAN

W e're only in Dallas for the weekend, and I had planned to show Bailey as much of my life as I could. However, after last night, I want to protect her more than ever before, and the idea of merging these two worlds is making me spiral. I won't let her see that though.

We spent the early morning in bed, initially just cuddling. I wasn't anticipating anything else, but she was eager to go as soon as my morning erection pressed into her.

Afterward, we showered and ordered some breakfast from a cafe near my building. While Bailey read her book in a chair by the window in my living room, I ran out to pick up the food and take Echo for a walk.

She's entranced in her book completely unaware of my presence, with her wavy auburn hair pulled to the side framing her face. She's in an oversized t-shirt, and cotton shorts that show off her curves. I stand there, admiring her for a few moments before I break the stillness.

"Waffles!" I say softly not to her startle her.

"Mmmm, yum!" She exclaims with a smile on her face.

"Echo, how was your walk my love?" Despite her deafness, Bailey speaks to her often, which I find adorable and endearing.

"What's the plan for the day?" She asks pulling a container out of the bag. Popping it open, she bends down to smell the food and gives a little moan that does something to my dick. *Stop it, she's hungry for the food, not you buddy.*

"Well, I thought I'd introduce you to my best friend Callum. We'll have lunch with him and his girl, Juniper."

"Is her name seriously Juniper? That's adorable."

I chuckle, "Yeah, I call her Junie and she hates it. They've been together for a few years now. I really think you'll love them."

"That's nice," she takes a bite and looks out the window. "So, do they know that you're bringing someone with you?"

"Of course. I told Callum about my plans before we left, and it was Junie's idea to meet for lunch."

She was apprehensive, but I did my best to re-assure her that she would have a nice time, and that they will adore her just as much as I do. I'm not concerned about them; it's my family that I am worried about more than anything.

After finishing breakfast, we spent the rest of the morning reading and relaxing with Echo before heading out.

Lunch with Callum and Juniper far exceed-ed my expectations. The girls shared their book boyfriends, and Juniper invited Bailey to join her online book club. They even exchanged numbers, which I'm quite certain is Juniper's attempt to steal Bailey away from me.

While the girls were engrossed in their conversations, Callum took the opportunity to share his thoughts about me introducing Bailey to my family. He expressed his concerns about the idea, suggesting that it *might* not be a good idea this soon in the relationship.

Callum has been my best friend since Middle School. Our families are very close, so he knows exactly what they are like, and what their standards are. His family isn't as rough around the edges as mine though, and I spent a lot of time over at their house growing up, attempting to get away from mine. His mom was like a second mom to me, and his father is so supportive and kind, I wondered how our dads were best friends.

The longer we talk about it, the more I begin to agree with Cal. I've never brought a girl home that I cared about this much, or at least not one I concerned myself with their opinion of.

Kyle is cold and calculated, while my father is judgmental and has little tolerance for those he considers less than himself. Even my older sister and mother are judgmental in their own ways. Despite their charity work with the homeless community, they lack the skills to engage with those in the lower and middle classes. I don't fault them for it, they have been one with the rich and fortunate for decades.

We finish up and say our goodbyes, the girls hug and promise to keep in touch. I take Bailey's hand as we turn to walk back to the car.

"Looks like you had a *horrible* time," I joke while nudging her with my elbow.

"Okay, you were right. Juniper is *amazing*. And Callum seems really nice," She smiles, gripping my hand tighter, and looping her other arm around mine.

"Thank you for bringing me."

"Than you for being willing to meet them. They mean the world to me and I'm glad y'all hit it off."

She closed mouth smiles up and me which makes her dimples extra noticeable, and I swear my heart does a backflip.

The fifteen-minute car ride back to the condo was filled with her recounting the conversations from lunch, and gawking over the city's sights.

Before we even make it back, Juniper had already sent her a text, inviting us to a rodeo in Houston tomorrow night.

She lit up as soon as she read it, and practically begged me to agree to take her. Of course, I can't deny my girl a rodeo while we're here.

We decide to plan a day of shopping tomorrow so she can get some boots and a hat for the event. Apparently those are a necessity.

⟫⟫⟫ ⟪⟪⟪

We're only home for an hour when I hear my phone go off, it's Kyle. I step outside onto the patio to take the call so Bailey can read in silence.

"Yeah?" I answer, leaning against the banister looking out towards the city skyline. There was a time where nothing could beat this view, but the mountain range is something else, and I can't wait to get back. Even the air is better, clearer there, I think to myself as I take a deep breath, preparing for what my brother has to say.

"Mom knows you're in town, a friends of hers saw you at The Brick with Callum, Juniper, and some girl."

Damn. I was hoping to avoid this. I know I had planned to stop in at some point while being here, but I didn't tell them I was in town just in case I changed my mind.

Dallas isn't a small town, the chances I was seen in public were astronomically low. Apparently the universe didn't care about those odds.

"Ok. And?" I say, turning to face the inside of my condo now. I know where this is headed and I'd really like to get this over with.

"And, she would like to see you. So would dad. They expect to see you at dinner tonight." He sighs. "There's some business to discuss. Oh. And bring the girl." Silence.

Fucker.

I saunter back inside. Bailey looks up and with one glance, she can see the tension on my face and the tightness in my chest.

"Who was that?" She asks softly, standing to walk towards me.

"My brother. Apparently they know I'm in town and want to see me tonight."

"Oh. Is that a bad thing?" She rests her hands over my fists that are balled up on the counter.

"Yes. They want me to bring you with me."

She looks at me and I can see the puzzled look and hint of pain in her eyes. She feels like I don't want them to meet her because of who she is, she thinks I'm ashamed of her.

Removing her hands from mine abruptly she says, "I'll stay here, I understand."

"No. You don't understand, Bailey. This has nothing to do with you and everything to do with them and who they are as people."

The room begins to spin, and my heart rate quickens. I don't want them to snuff out her light, or make her feel unworthy of being with me. She just gave all of herself to me, and I don't need her doubting her worth again, or more than she already does. Once they catch a glimpse of her, or hear about her life in Colorado, that's precisely what they'll do. Apart from Tasha, my entire family is composed of pretentious assholes.

With that, my phone vibrates again. Mom. I slide my phone across the counter away from me, and lower myself to the bar stool. I can sense a panic attack coming on. Sometimes, they strike without warning, but I've been on the verge of one since we arrived in Dallas. Somehow I've managed to push it down up until now. Now, the pressure is building, and I'm hyperventilating.

"Rylan, come with me," Bailey is holding my hand, walking me through the bedroom and towards the bathroom. My vision is tunneling and my breath is unsteady. I feel like I'm going to pass out if I don't sit down soon.

"Focus on my voice, Rylan." She says softy. Turning on the shower, she pulls us through the threshold once she's sure the temperature is satisfactory.

I can't recall the moment when I transitioned from standing to lying down. We're on the shower floor, enveloped in the gentle, calming flow of the water. She leans against the wall, and I find my head nestled in her lap. Her fingers softly caress my hair as she hums a soothing tune. I've never been able to come out of an anxiety attack this quickly, and without medication before.

I remain in this position until I am certain that the situation has passed. Once it has, I gradually sit up to meet her gaze. "I'm sorry," I utter, infusing my voice with a subtle tinge of shame and embarrassment.

"You have nothing to apologize for, I have anxiety attacks, too," She reaches out to move a strand of my hair from my forehead, "I understand."

Sitting fully clothed beneath the water, completely vulnerable to her, I've never experienced a deeper level of intimacy with anyone than I do with her now in this moment.

She's utter perfection, and she belongs to me.

Chapter Eighteen

BAILEY

Once I was sure that Rylan felt grounded again I switched off the shower, and quickly retrieved towels and a change of clothes for each of us. We agreed it wasn't worth the turmoil to see his family, and decided to order in some Chinese takeout and watch movies the rest of the day instead.

There was no pressure to act a certain way or engage in conversation; most of the night was spent in comfortable silence, simply being in each other's presence.

The following day we woke up early and did some light shopping before it was time to meet Callum and Juniper at the rodeo. The drive to Houston from Dallas was about four hours, so we had to leave pretty early to get there in decent time.

Standing at the entrance, waiting for us, was Callum and Juniper. Callum was wearing blue jeans, cowboy boots, a blue flannel shirt, and a black cowboy hat. He's handsome with rich brown eyes, dark brown hair that's slightly shorter than Rylan's, and he's covered in tattoos. Juniper wore an adorable short white dress with cowgirl boots and a cowgirl hat over her bright red hair. She has the cutest freckles and the brightest green eyes I've ever seen.

I could tell Rylan had no desire to be here at first, but I'm thankful he ultimately decided to join us.

Callum unveiled a side of Rylan that I thoroughly enjoyed watching, he became carefree and there was a lightness to him.

At one point Rylan had jumped up onto Callum's back, wrapping his legs around him with one arm around his neck, and the other outstretched above them, waving around his cowboy hat. Then Callum began bucking and running around playfully with him on his back, and I absolutely made sure to capture the whole thing on video.

Rylan doesn't have to conceal the aspect of his family life with Callum, he doesn't have to shield him from it or present a false persona and can completely be himself around him. I genuinely hope that one day he can experience that true sense of freedom and comfort with me well, but I understand that it won't happen until he's prepared to confront his family, and take the necessary steps to heal from the traumas they've inflicted upon him.

Walking through the event center, I was captivated by the dazzling lights and enthralling sounds. The intriguing blend of aromas, including the delicious scent of fried food and the earthy aroma of the livestock, creating an intoxicating atmosphere. Juniper interlocked our arms and began skipping, guiding me through the sea of people and leading me to our reserved seats.

Naturally, we had been granted prime seating, a testament to the boys' unwavering commitment to providing an exceptional experience for us tonight. They spared no expense and I'm not complaining one bit. I would never have been able to access seats like this if it weren't for them.

The rodeo was everything I had hoped for and more. There was music, dancing, thrilling barrel racing, and heart-stopping bull riding. Although we have a similar rodeo back home, albeit on a smaller scale, I couldn't help but feel a sense of pride in being here.

My favorite part of the night, apart from simply being with the people I was with, was watching the Mutton Busting portion of the event. It's where toddlers and young children buck around on sheep, and hold on as long as they can. It was equally hilarious and adorable, and Juniper squealed at the sight while tugging on Callum's arm, begging him to put a baby in her so their child can grow up and be a part of it.

We indulged in various themed food and drinks, and watched the fireworks at the end of the event before making our way back to Dallas. I didn't want the night to end, it was absolute perfection and I could really see myself becoming a part of their group.

Rylan held me and leaned down to kiss me often during the fireworks show, and Juniper snagged the sweetest photo of us from a perfect angle that doesn't make me cringe or hate the way I look. She's already sent it to me, along with some selfies we took together, and it takes everything in me not to make the photo of me and Rylan my Lock Screen background like a teenager in love.

The return trip was slightly shorter, which I was extremely thankful for as Echo probably needed to go outside, and I was feeling the exhaustion from all the excitement of the evening start to overcome me.

Throughout the drive, Rylan had his hand on my thigh or in my hand, and would occasionally look over at me and stare longer than I felt was safe for him to do so while driving.

He's making me fall for him, damnit. A part of me doesn't want to go back to Colorado, fearing that things will go back to how they were or that this was just us living on a vacation high.

We've been back in Elk Hollow for a few weeks now, and I've more or less spent every night with Rylan since being back. Thankfully, my concerns of the dynamic changing once we retuned to our every day life was just my paranoia and anxiety talking.

We haven't exactly had a conversation about putting a label on whatever this is between us, but I would say this is the closest to being in a serious relationship I've ever been. Rylan displays signs of being extremely possessive over me, but I feel that there's something holding him back from fully committing.

I'm positive it's his family, and the fact that he despises his career, but I don't want to upset him by bringing it up.

For now, I'll relish in what we have, and remain hopeful for what we could have in the future.

Chapter Nineteen

RYLAN

I woke up to a phone call from my brother this morning, I didn't want to answer but he kept calling until I finally did.

Of fucking course my brother would pull this bull-shit. I'm so incredibly sick of the way this family handles things, and this is exactly why I want out. Someone else makes a mistake, and I am immediately expected to drop what I'm doing to help save the company, but more importantly Dad's ass.

I was told that someone had dropped the ball somewhere with this deal here in Elk Hollow, even though I know for a fact everything that was left up to me was handled accordingly, but now I need to head to Dallas for fuck knows how long to remedy shit.

We've been back for about a month now, and things have been going exceptionally well with Bailey. We've discovered a routine that suits both of us, and she's even allowed me to become a part of her personal life.

We now double date with Aspen and Micah every weekend, and have dinner once a week with Rob and Sandy.

It's very domestic of us, and not my typical style but I can't see myself ever going back to dating without intent.

Or dating anyone that isn't Bailey.

After sitting on this news and his request (read demand) for a few hours, I decide to give my brother a return call. I really don't want to disrupt my life here right now if I can avoid it.

"Hey Kyle, is there anyway I can stay here?" I don't typically enjoy calling him, but I know that if I were to text him, he'd probably ignore it.

"No, we didn't want to tell you over the phone, but Dad isn't doing well."

"So there isn't a problem with the deal? Why the fuck wouldn't you tell me this sooner?" I ask, a tinge of guilt rushing through me.

No, my dad isn't my favorite person, but they not only lied to me, but there's something wrong with our father and I'm just now finding out.

I sigh, "I'll be home tomorrow."

Silence. Again, the bastard hung up without saying anything.

Why am I surprised every time he does that?

I drive into town to stop at Brews N Booze for a midday pick me up, and to ask Bailey what she wants to do for dinner tonight.

She's going to understand why I'm leaving, probably a little too much, she is close with her family and struggles grasping how things with mine can be so rough and seemingly irreconcilable.

Stepping into the shop, I'm hit with the scent of freshly brewed coffee and something sweet.

I hope they got a batch of that lemon loaf with the icing on the tops today, those are my current guilty pleasure.

Bailey is leaning against this side of the counter, taking inventory of the bagged whole beans in a basket, and talking to Aspen who is on the opposite side. I take a quick look around and when I see that there are no customers around to see me, I slap her ass and squeeze firmly.

"Rylan!" She shouts out, spinning around to reach my gaze.

I don't think she wants to feel amused, but I can see the smile she's attempting to hide behind the scowl.

"Well hello there Bailey Boo," I wink at her and turn to Aspen.

"And hello to you, too, tree." Aspen gives an eye roll and flips me off before turning to pour me some coffee.

"Very funny, *Ryan*." She quips.

We don't dislike each other, in fact she reminds me of my sister Natasha. It's easy to joke around with her. I can't help that she's named after a tree, and she can't help that my name was mistaken for Ryan.

Bailey giggles and smiles wide. I know that she's happy her best friend and I are able to get along.

"We still on for dinner?"

"Yep, I'll be off in two hours."

"What would you like? Please don't say the diner, I don't think I could eat another meal there this week." I say patting my stomach.

"I think I've put on about fifteen pounds since moving here."

Bailey scoffs and elbows me in the stomach, "Yeah, right. I think you're going to be just fine. Surprise me, I don't care."

"You're so easy to please. How did I get so lucky?" I say batting my eyes at her before wrapping my arms around her and kissing the top of her head.

I pay for my coffee and lemon loaf, give her a kiss, and let her know that I'll be at my house with Echo when she's ready to come over.

On my days off I keep Echo with me so she isn't alone while Bailey is busy.

It's almost like we have shared custody, and it makes me wonder for a quick second what it would look like to have a kid together someday.

I settled on parmesan crusted cod with roasted carrots and sweet potatoes. I've made it for her before and I know she enjoys it. I also bought her a carton of her favorite ice cream, Monkey something or other; it's banana flavored with walnuts and chocolate chunks. She's obsessed but I find the artificial banana flavor repulsive.

I don't need to pack a suitcase since a lot of my stuff is still back home, but I've packed a duffel bag with my laptop, chargers, the book I've been reading, and a few other essentials. It's by the front door and Bailey takes note of it as soon as she steps into the house.

"Going somewhere?" She asks as she kneels down to take her shoes off.

"I spoke to my brother today. Apparently our father isn't doing well, so I'm flying out in the morning."

"Oh my God! I'm so sorry!!" She makes her way over to me, wrapping her hands around my neck and getting on her tip toes to give me a kiss. She knows my relationship with my father is rocky at best, so she doesn't seem surprised when I don't say anything else on the matter.

We sit in silence for most of dinner, I'm trying not to let my heightened emotions towards my family affect things with Bailey, but she can sense things are off. It's not until I present her with her ice cream and ask if she wants to watch the romcom she's been bugging me about for weeks now that she perks up, and the mood lightens.

Before we head off to bed, she approaches me cautiously, "Let me come with you," She says.

I feel a glimmer of relief at the thought of her being with me. The first time I had an anxiety attack in her presence, she managed to calm me down much faster than any other method I've used in the past. Before I can overthink things, I quickly respond with a resounding yes, and she's off calling Vy to inform her about a family emergency that will keep from work for a few days.

Once we landed, I instructed the driver to take us straight to my parents', wanting to get this over with.

I was apprehensive about bringing Bailey along, but I carefully considered the pros and cons. I have hope that, given the circumstances, they won't feel compelled to interfere in my personal matters too much and be cordial with Bailey at most.

As we pulled around the circle drive in front of their one-story mini mansion, Bailey is captivated by the grounds and estate. Her mouth hangs open as we ascend the steps leading up to the grand double doors.

I place my arm around her waist and gently squeeze, prompting her to look up at me. I can sense her apprehension, but she's putting her own concerns aside for me. These aren't the ideal circumstances for introducing her to them, nevertheless, I'm glad she's here.

I ring the doorbell, and Mr. Kingsley, their devoted butler arrives to greet us. He's been with my family since childhood, and I've always respected him. A half-smile graces his lips as he recognizes me, and he extends his hand for mine. I scoff and reach out to embrace him in a hug before turning to introduce him to Bailey, who stands behind me unsure of how to react.

"Mr. Sterling, Ms. Collins, please come in," he says holding his frail arm out to invite us in. "What brings you by this afternoon? I wasn't made aware that they would be expecting you today." He says as he leads us into the main sitting room.

"What do you mean you weren't expecting me? Kyle called me yesterday and told me I needed to come home, that my father was ill?" I begin glancing around, no sign of anyone and there were no extra cars in the driveway. "Where is Adam, Mr. Kingsley?"

He appears confused, and I can sense that he's hesitant to say something that my parents might disapprove of. As I'm about to instruct him to re-spond to my questions, my mother unexpectedly makes her presence known.

"Rylan, you're home! Oh, I didn't expect this. What brings you by?" Her long, loose-curled blond hair frames her face, and her slim build is accentuated by the summer dress adorned with roses, paired with a pair of black high heels, pearl earrings, and a gold necklace.

"Where is Dad?" I growl in response, knowing damn well they've set me up and he's perfectly fine.

"Now Rylan, don't overreact. Your father and brother knew you wouldn't come unless they fibbed a little." Pushing her hair to one side of her head, and lowering herself to sit on the arm of the couch, "Please don't make a big deal of this."

"We're leaving." I turn to grab Bailey's hand and lead her out of here when my father makes his way into the room from his study. "Rylan, just the man I was looking for. Kyle will be here soon. Please, sit."

"No," I say, fighting the urge to punch him in the face. "Kyle made me believe something was wrong with you, and now that I see you're perfectly fine, we're leaving." Holding a very timid Bailey's hand we are almost to the door when Adam calls out to us, "Please, at least meet us here for dinner tonight. Seven o' clock. I promise, we won't bother you again if you come. Both of you."

I reluctantly agree to join them for dinner, despite the growing anger inside of me. I don't understand why they decided to deceive me, or what their pre-rogative is, but I want to end this ordeal and return to Colorado as soon as possible.

During the drive to my condo, Bailey remains quiet, but she sits beside me with her hand on my knee and her head resting on my shoulder. She understands that I'm not in the mood to talk, and I appreciate her sensitivity and awareness of my needs without me having to express them.

I understand that we'll need to discuss her attire for tonight. Unfortunately, none of her current outfits are suitable for my family's formal dinner, which I dread having to bring up. During the drive, I search for places that can accommodate her size and offer formal wear. I'm aware that being plus-size can make shopping challenging for her, and I don't want to disappoint her by choosing a venue where she can't find anything. However, I also don't want to offend her by selecting a place exclusively designed for larger women.

I give up and decide to text Junie to inform her that we'll be in town for a few days, and ask if she could meet with Bailey today to help her choose an outfit for dinner.

Fortunately, she agrees and is familiar with nearby clothing stores that will be accommodating to Bailey, considering her own slightly thicker build. She also suggests that I stay behind with Cal, so Bailey doesn't feel awkward shopping for clothes with me as her audience.

Juniper is well-versed in our family's expectations, having been involved in numerous events organized by the Sterlings. Callum is a childhood friend, and our families are exceptionally close, so Junie understands what attire is considered appropriate.

Chapter Twenty

BAILEY

Being at Rylan's childhood home with his parents, was an overwhelming and terrifying experience to say the least.

When he recounts stories to me, I can't help but imagine them as Emily and Richard Gilmore from Gilmore Girls.

While the resemblance is not entirely accurate, they posses a level of fear inducing judgment that is not incomparable. The mere thought of having dinner with them tonight sends shivers down my spine.

Rylan didn't want to, and I understand it was uncomfortable for him to mention, but I need to buy a formal outfit for tonight. I'm not upset about it; he's right, what I brought with me is leggings, jeans, and T-shirts. Nothing that I'm sure either of his parents own themselves.

I'm relieved that Juniper will be accompanying me shopping instead of Rylan. It makes me feel more at ease, and I've definitely missed her. We text almost daily and have become fast friends. I just know she would get along well with Aspen, and

I'm desperately hoping that I can convince her and Callum to move to Colorado eventually.

"June Bug and Cal will be here in about an hour," Rylan informs as he strolls shirtless through the kitchen of his condo.

He's just finished taking a shower and his hair is still dripping wet, cascading droplets down his face and onto his bare chest. Ugh, I find it irresistible when his hair falls in front of his forehead like this, and I want to reach out and run my hands through it.

He notices my staring, and wriggles his eyebrows at me, "Want a piece of this?" He quips endearingly with the most ridiculous smile across his face.

"You wish," I joke, sitting on the kitchen counter, licking a glob of peanut butter off of a spoon.

Before I can react, he stands in front of me, his hands push my legs that dangle off the counter apart, as his body wedges in between them. His hands travel up and down my thighs, and his mouth peppers soft kisses along my neck and shoulder.

He smells like his body wash, a woodsy evergreen and sandalwood scent, it's intoxicating.

His hands begin to travel up to my warm center and I spread my thighs further apart ever so slightly as my breath quickens, allowing him access. I'm instantly wet and tingling.

"I remember the first night we spent here," He whispers into my ear and biting my earlobe.

"The way you came for me, gave all of yourself to me for the first time. I want to feel that again."

I toss the spoon into the sink next to us and wrap my arms around his neck. Leaning my head to the side, I begin to kiss his neck in return before biting him, marking him with my teeth and whispering into his ear, "Then take it, take me."

With that he growls, and despite my weight, he places his hands underneath my ass and lifts me off of the counter. I squeal in shock and demand that he set me down before he drops me or hurts himself.

"I've got you Bailey," He says as he carries me through to his room and drops me gently onto his bed. "Strip," He commands.

Mere seconds pass before we are both undressed and he's towering over me on the mattress. With one hand stretched in front of him, his fingers teasing my slit, "You're so wet for me already, baby." He growls.

"Let me taste you," I say breathlessly as he growls and slides off me.

He guides me to my knees as he stands in front of me, holding my head and wrapping his fingers into my hair.

I start off slow, kissing him, running my hands all over him, exploring every inch, licking the pre come off his tip before sucking his thick length into my mouth, sliding him as deep as I can go without gagging. One hand gripping the base of his shaft, while the other cradles and lightly squeezes his balls, he grunts and rocks his pelvis into me. This goes on for a while before he grips tighter and groans.

"I'm going to come, Bailey," He says as we transition into a quicker, more frantic rhythm.

I feel like I'm going to gag but I don't stop, running my tongue along his length. He begins to pulse inside of me, his warm liquid rushing down my throat. It's sweet and salty, and I love every bit of it, ensuring I swallow every last drop.

Once he's finished, he snaps me up and our mouths clash together, he can taste himself on my lips and it makes me feel even more aroused than I thought possible.

He pushes me back onto the bed, and slides his body down mine, caressing every inch of it on his way down, with one hand on my breast, flicking the hardened bud and pressing it between two fingers as he slides and pushes his tongue into me, sending my body into convulsions almost instantly.

My back arches every time he thrusts his fingers inside of me as he grazes my clit with his tongue. My breath shudders and my insides plead for him.

His cock is hard again and growing more with each second that passes. Coming up from my center, he leans down to kiss me before his tongue moves down and begins circling my nipple.

I dig my fingernails into his biceps, dragging them down the length of his arms to his wrists. It sends him into a frenzy and he's suddenly ripping the condom out of the wrapper, lining himself up, and thrusting into me with a great force, bottoming out and making me whimper and cry out. He doesn't stop, as he's grown accustomed to my sounds and he knows he isn't truly hurting me. Which is good, because if he were to stop right now, I'd lose it.

After a few more pumps, he vigorously flips me onto my stomach, lifts my pelvis, and parts my thighs, positioning himself right up against me again. Slapping and grabbing my ass, he grunts before inviting himself back inside from behind. My pussy is drenched and this angle is hitting points I've never felt before, sending me into a pool of ecstasy.

Our bodies slapping together, my head bobbing with every thrust. He has one hand braced on my lower back and the other on my ass, slapping and squeezing with every few pumps.

"I'm going to come," I shout out to him, knowing that statement will send him to the brink as well. He reaches around and pinches and fondles my clit. I pulse and tighten around his thick length as he grunts and digs his fingers into my love handles, holding onto them like if he were to let go, I'd fall away from him.

Our pace quickens, I hold my breath and he sends me into a screaming orgasm that makes me collapse. With my head on my arms on top of the pillow and only my ass in the air being held up by him, I can feel him twitching inside of me as he starts to go limp.

He slowly begins to pull himself out, and stands to tie off the condom before making his way to the bathroom to toss it into the waste bin. I hear the shower spit on, and he emerges with my robe and holds his hand out for me, helping me to my feet.

"Junie and Cal will be here soon, we should probably get cleaned up," He says, pulling me into him, kissing me passionately and pushing the hair from my face.

I think I'm falling in love with Rylan Caine Sterling, and that realization is equally terrifying and beautiful.

Chapter Twenty-One

RYLAN

D espite the rocky start to our morning with my parents, the rest of the day has been going pleasantly well. After devouring every inch of Bailey before Juniper and Callum arrived, we took another shower with minutes to spare.

While the girls are shopping, Callum and I are at his art studio a couple of blocks away, preparing for an event that he is hosting tonight. I told him that Bailey and I would try to be here for it if we wrap things up at my parents as quickly as I hope to.

"You nervous for tonight, bro?" Callum asks as he places an event sign on an easel at the front of the gallery.

"I mean, I'm more pissed than anything. I don't really know what to expect, and I just want to keep Bailey from them."

"If you've got feelings for this girl, like I think you do, you wont be able to keep them separated forever." He has a point, I shrug. "Yeah, well I'm still not happy about it.

"Do you think you know why they might've convinced you to come out here?"

"Nope," I say popping the P.

We've finished setting up and are now going back and forth guessing why they tricked me into returning here for them while waiting for the girls to finish shopping. Juniper will drop Bailey off at the studio fully ready, and we can head to my parents' from here. I brought my suit and have already changed into it in their apartment loft that's above the studio.

It's nearing six o'clock and my nerves are starting to get the best of me. Dinner is at seven and it's about a twenty minute drive. Now is not the time for Bailey to be late like she usually is. As soon as I reach for my phone to call her, I see Juniper walking through the front door of their apartment.

"You ready to see the most beautiful woman in the world?" She asks excitedly and proudly.

Behind her, Bailey pushes through the door and my jaw drops instantly. I've always thought she was beautiful, but this is another level. She's exuding confidence and it's beyond sexy.

Her dark auburn hair is curled tightly and cascades down her chest. She's wearing a stunning black full-length cocktail dress with a v-neckline that tastefully reveals her breasts. The dress has spaghetti straps and a large slit on the side of her leg that elegantly reveals some of her thigh, and the train is adorned with tulle fabric.

She twirls like a princess while Juniper rattles off everything that's featured within her outfit, and has her strutting down the hallway as if it were a runway built specifically for her. Thankfully, she's not wearing high heels, my girl may look graceful on the outside right now, but she is clumsy as hell.

"My God," I'm in disbelief as I approach her.

"You are the most beautiful woman in the world, Juniper wasn't exaggerating."

I'm finding it hard to keep my hands off of her, my fingers tracing the lines of her body, my eyes taking all of her in.

Ahem Callum clears his throat, "I think you guys are going to be late if you keep trying to undress her in my living room."

Bailey cackles and shyly attempts to hide her blushing face behind her coin purse.

"You do look lovely, Bails," Callum says while placing a kiss to her cheek.

"Doesn't she? I about *died* when she came out of the dressing room in this dress! Ahh, I'm obsessed!" Juniper adds while jumping up and down clapping her hands.

The girls hug goodbye and we head out into the darkness.

I don't even care how tonight goes with my family, as long as it ends with me getting Bailey out of this dress and underneath me.

Arriving at my parents' house for dinner on time was an unexpected surprise, but I felt a sense of relief wash over me. As I pulled into the circle drive, I recognized most of the vehicles, except for one.

Of course, Kyle, Rachel, Daniel, and the kids were here. However, I couldn't shake the feeling of suspicion about the mysterious red corvette parked among the familiar cars. They hadn't mentioned a business meeting scheduled for tonight, and if there was one, I couldn't understand why Bailey was expected to attend.

As we make our way into the dining area, the room falls silent. I have my hand placed firmly on Bailey's lower back, keeping her close and letting them witness that she is mine and I am proud of it.

"Well, brother. Glad you could make it." Kyle tips his glass to me.

"Yes, so nice to see you again son," My father interjects.

"Ry, you're looking healthy," Rachel adds coyly as Daniel stands to shake my hand and introduce himself to Bailey. So far he is the only one that has introduced himself to her, or even acknowledged her existence, but his lips are tight and his eyes look apologetic.

"Rylan. Caine. Sterling," I hear shriek from behind me "You are just as handsome as you were the day I met you!" Fuck, I recognize that high pitched preppy voice.

Dropping my hand from Bailey, I turn to see my ex-girlfriend, and family friend, Jessica. She's tall and thin wearing a bright red knee length dress that is so tight, it looks like it would bust open if she bent over, and her silicone DD sized breasts that do not fit the rest of her body, are practically falling out of the cups.

She has long bleached blond hair that goes down to her ass, and striking green eyes. She's a model and social media influencer, and our parents are best friends. We only dated exclusively for about a year on and off, but unfortunately she was always the one I turned to for a hookup, and the last time was before I moved out to Colorado. I should have known that was her corvette outside. She's always been a flashy one.

"Jessica," I say in a low growl. "What brings you to the Sterling family dinner?"

"Your father invited me, silly! You know how much Adam loves me and wishes you'd marry me already." She winks. Gross.

I glance over at Bailey who is standing there frozen, her eyes becoming glossy as she scans Jessica in front of her. Fuck I need to do something.

"Well now Jessica, you know that's not going to happen. I'm not attracted to snobby females that chase money and clout."

"You weren't saying that a few months ago when I was in your bed, babe." She says seductively as she brushes her hand across my chest and grabs my tie.

"Rylan, you know that you and Jessica belong together, that's why I invited her here tonight. She's more your speed," My father adds.

Bailey makes a sound, thanks my family for the invite, and quickly rushes out.

I grab Jessica's wrist and snatch it off of me. Holding her wrist tightly in my hand, I step to her, "You're nothing to me, and you never will be." I say before dropping her hand.

"Fuck all of you." I say as I march out of the room and begin searching for Bailey.

"Mr. Sterling?" Mr. Kingsley calls out to me from the entrance of the study. "I believe Ms. Collins is outside. She has called for a car service, sir."

"Shit, thank you Howard. Have a good evening."

"You as well, sir." He responds with a soft, apologetic tone. He would never speak out against my parents, or any of my family members, but I know he's a good man, and I know he genuinely feels awful about what transpired here.

"Bailey?" I make my way towards my car that she's leaned up against. Crying. Shit.

"I am so sorry, I don't know why they invited her, and I told her off immediately. She had no right."

"A couple of months ago, Rylan?" She can barely look me in the eyes.

"It was before I moved to Colorado, I promise."

"But, you were with her not much sooner than you pursued me. Is it that easy for you to bounce from one girl to another? Your father is probably right anyways."

"No," I say reaching for her hand. "It's not like that. Please, let me explain."

Just then a car pulls up and she pushes past me, making her way towards it.

"This is my ride, I'm going to meet Juniper and she'll take me to the airport tomorrow."

"Please. Please don't go, come back to the condo with me." Searching her eyes for any sign that she will be receptive to me, I see nothing, she just looks broken. Beautiful, and broken.

"I need space. Please let me go." Everything in me screams to prevent her from leaving, but I can't. I watch her climb into the ride-share and drive off my parents' property. It takes all my strength not to rush back into the house and knock my father out. What the hell was he thinking?

I begin to drive home, but find myself heading to the art studio instead, knowing that's where Bailey is going to be. I understand that she needs some space, but I can't bear the thought of her walking away from me like this. She needs to know that I had nothing to do with it, she has to trust me.

Callum is standing at the gallery's entrance, greeting guests that are arriving for the event. I attempt to avoid him, but he spots me and promptly excuses himself to meet me.

"You can't be here right now, Ry," He says hushed under his breath as he nods and smiles to guests while they file in through the doors behind me.

"She doesn't want to see you, and you know Juniper; she'll cut a bitch for someone she cares about. If she sees you, she'll pounce."

"Cal, I have to talk to her, you don't understand."

"Jessica, right? I think I got the gist."

He turns to shake someones hand, then snaps his attention back to me. "You have some serious damage control to do, but not here, not tonight. Please, Ry. You need to let her have space. She's safe here." He places his hand on my shoulder, "I love you, but I'm so sick of your family, bro. Figure shit out before you fuck up the best thing that's ever happened to you."

I watch as he heads back to his post, knowing Bailey is right above me, probably broken into a million pieces; feeling embarrassed and ashamed. There's nothing I can do to mend her broken heart right now and it makes me want to break everything in sight, but I also know that Callum is right. She is safe here, and she does need space. But that doesn't stop me from sending her a text later before I head to bed. Alone.

> I'm so sorry Bailey. You looked stunning in that dress. Goodnight.

There was so much more that I wanted to say, so much more that I wanted to do. Fuck my family, and fuck Jessica. Yeah Ry, fucking her is what got you into this situation in the first place. I switch the light off and toss and turn all night, wondering if she's awake, too.

Chapter Twenty-Two

BAILEY

I understand that I'm being irrational, and it wasn't Rylan's fault what transpired last night with his parents and that bimbo super model. It was easier to lash out at him, especially when I could only compare it to the intense feelings I had when Anthony slept with Liz, but ten times worse.

The intensity of my feelings for Rylan is undeniable, surpassing anything I've ever felt for anyone else. I know I'm falling in love with him, and that's terrifying to me.

Last night was hell. Juniper helped me out of my dress when I couldn't breathe from the anxiety attack I was having, and I spent most of the evening upstairs on the floor of their apartment bathroom crying. Juniper went to pick up my extra clothes from Rylan's, and she missed all of the event that was being held at their studio which of course made me feel even more awful.

When I woke up this morning to a text from him, I admit I wanted to text him back immediately. I wanted to ask him to come pick me up and fly back to Colorado together and forget everything that had happened. But Juniper is right, we're both too emotional right now to have a serious conversation with each other without the risk of saying something we might regret.

Callum paid for my flight home which I offered to pay him back for, but he declined. Stating Rylan would kick his ass if he knew that they let me pay for my own ticket.

Aspen is going to pick me up at the Denver airpot when I land. I didn't give her too many details, but she knows I left with Rylan and am returning without him. We'll have plenty of time to go over all the painful details on the drive back to Elk Hollow from the airport though.

> I just wanted to let you know that I got a flight home. Aspen is meeting me there. Fly safe.

I understand I shouldn't have texted him, but informing him that I'm not stranded is different from texting him to discuss what happened last night. I hadn't received a text back before boarding, or when I landed in Denver and turned my phone off airplane mode. I wish he had his location enabled so I could see where he is. I have no idea what his itinerary looked like, or if he was even returning today.

I begin to lose my composure when I see Aspen pull up to the arrivals terminal, knowing that I'm going to have to recount last nights events for a second time, and feeling safe enough to let myself feel all of the feelings again once I see her face.

"This bitch said what? She put her hands where?" Aspen shouts, almost swerving in the lane to our right as she snaps her neck towards me, looking for the confirmation on my face.

"I will *bury* her."

"It's fine, really." I say, looking out the window, watching the scenery pass by. "She was really hot though."

"Girl, she sounds like a hoe. Her personality makes her ugly as fuck, trust me."

"She was hot enough for Rylan to sleep with, and her dad seems to think she's better for him than me. I have a feeling they have a very long history, and he's probably right."

"Girl, *you* are hot enough for Rylan to sleep with, so stop with that. Would you feel better if I kicked him in the kneecaps next time I saw him, though? Cause I'll do it for you."

It makes me giggle a little to picture her kicking him, but I let her know it's not necessary.

By the time we arrive at the duplex, it's already dark, and I'm eager to get inside, take a shower, and get some rest.

Fortunately, I don't have to return to work for another day, so I can take my time to compose myself and catch up on sleep. I don't notice Rylan's truck parked in front, and I still haven't heard back from him. I try to stay calm and not worry excessively, but I can't help but feel a sense of unease and concern. I genuinely hope that he has also just needed space, and I'm hopeful that I'll either hear from or see him tomorrow.

Rylan

When I noticed Bailey's text message while I was preparing to head to the airport, I felt a sense of relief. However, her message felt cold and detached, which hurt. I had every intention of boarding that flight and going straight to her house to talk to her. Nevertheless, a persistent nagging feeling held me back from doing just that.

I am responsible for her pain, and the thought of seeing her in that state again would be devastating for me. I am well aware of my own flaws, as well as my families, and the impact they can have on others, but this was a new low even for them.

I took a later flight to ensure Bailey was home and asleep by the time I arrived from Denver around one in the morning. If we intend to discuss things right away, I needed to formulate my thoughts, and I felt that we'd have a much more productive conversation if we both had a full night's rest.

I saw your truck when I took Echo out, glad you made it back safe... I'm sorry about how I reacted. Can we talk?

Yeah, we probably should. I'll be over in 20?

Sounds great, see you soon! :)

I hate that she appears excited about my agreeing to come talk to her. I spent most of the drive up here contemplating what I would say.

When I woke up this morning, I felt pretty confident in my decision, although the thought of leaving her and returning home is excruciating. Witnessing her pain due to my family and myself, followed by her effortless forgiveness and readiness to resume our relationship as if nothing transpired, makes me nervous.

I've never had a serious relationship where I had to genuinely consider someone else's emotions, or the impact of my words and actions, or my family's. I'm positive that she'll get hurt again if I stay. She'll let me hurt her, and she'll keep forgiving me. That can't happen.

Walking up to her front door, I'm greeted by the sweet melody of her singing along to one of her favorite songs, Right Though Me by The Home Team. As I take a peek through the window, I'm captivated by the sight of her dancing in the kitchen with Echo perched on her hind legs, and her paws clasped in her hands. The heartache intensifies with each passing moment that I continue to let myself watch.

Thankfully, she sees me looking in and signals for me to enter, dropping Echo's paws and turning down the music.

"Good morning, how was your drive?" She looks good, she looks happy.

"It was alright, yours?

"Same. Wanna sit? I made coffee!" She says cheerfully, fuckin hell this is going to suck.

"Uhh, sure. I'm not planning on staying long though." I say as I go to pull out a chair as she hands me a cup of coffee.

"Oh? Okay-"

"Look, I'm sorry about what happened at my parents' house. It was uncalled for, and they did it intentionally because they have set standards for themselves, their children, and those they choose to associate with. It had nothing to do with you, and everything to do with them."

"I understand, Rylan." She says, reaching for my hands that I pull away and place in my lap.

"What they think of you, is not what I think of you. But I do know that you deserve better than me. What you saw, is what you get. What you'd always get. Nothing is going to change, and I can't let you be a part of that."

"Are you sure you don't feel the same way they do? Because you're acting like them right now." Her voice steady, and with a tinge of anger now.

"Bailey, I'm sorry. I need to leave."

"I love you, Rylan. And I thought you loved me, too."

Fuck, I wasn't expecting her to utter those words to me, we've never said them aloud before. However, she's not mistaken; I've felt that way for her since the moment she sat in the shower with me while I was having a panic attack. She knew exactly what I needed, and how to help me. She didn't pass judgement, and it was the most intimate experience I have ever shared with anyone.

I go to stand, "I'm sorry, Bailey. This is for the better. Please try to understand."

With that, I start walking towards the door. She doesn't chase or call out to me, but I can hear her stifling a sob behind her hand, trying to keep me from hearing her.

As soon as the door closes behind me, I sink to the ground, leaning against the door. Her crying has become much louder now, and my heart is breaking into a million pieces.

I left her to protect her from further harm, but here we are. There was no way to win this situation.

Chapter Twenty-Three

BAILEY

I 'm unable to eat, sleep, or move from my bed. This is unlike any heartbreak I've experienced before. When Rylan left my house after expressing my love for him, it felt like he took my heart with him.

He hopped into his truck and hasn't come back. All I have the energy and motivation for is work and lying in bed, and I can't comprehend how things changed so rapidly.

We were on top of the world, and then in an instant, everything changed. I was contemplating the end of our relationship one moment, and then in the next, he was ending things with me. I feel like I have a serious case of whiplash on top of a broken heart.

Even Echo is acting differently. I know she senses my severe mood shift, but it's more than that. She got used to having Rylan around every day, playing with her and taking her for walks as well. He became another one of her people, and I often find her staring at the front door, even when Aspen and I are home.

It's already been about a week since he walked out of my front door, and subsequently my life, but it feels like it happened just yesterday. Juniper says he's back in town, but is refusing to see anyone. Callum went over yesterday to check on him as he has an extra key to his place, but he locked the bedroom door and wouldn't open it for him. After about an hour, Cal gave up and went home. He said his place is darker than usual, and messy, which is very unlike Rylan.

I would be lying if I said that I didn't feel a little happy to hear that he is miserable as well. However, the feeling didn't last long, because ultimately I do love him, and I want him to find peace and be happy with his life even if it's not with me.

I did some light internet stalking on Jessica, I got her info from Juniper even though she begged me not to give her the time of day, I couldn't help myself. Turns out, everyone was right about her. She bounces from guy to guy, hooking up with whoever appears to have the most money, and is willing to spend it on her. She has a new fling every few months. Rylan was no exception, she doesn't love him, she loves his families money and power.

The few photos she has with him over the past few years, he doesn't look nearly as happy or himself as he does in the few photos I have of him, and with him. Which gives me a glimmer of hope that things between us is real, and he just needs to work on himself. But hell, it would be really hard to just let him back in after this, even as hard as it is not having him in my life right now.

We've officially entered the hottest month of the year here; August. Days even up here on the mountain get to be in the low eighties. I can't complain though, because back in Denver their high temperatures reach closer to 100 degrees.

Violet is out of town for a rodeo this weekend, and when she attends events out of town, she closes the coffee shop. Most of the locals don't put up too much of a fight over it, as long as Brick or Micah are there to keep the bar open at night, people can live without their coffee. This means that I also have the weekend off.

Brick is taking over the bar for Micah so he can take Aspen to Denver for a concert and to stay with some friends. They invited me to come with them, but I felt like my depression couldn't thrive in that kind of environment, and in order for me to successfully get through this, I need to couch rot a little longer with Ben and Jerry's ice cream and romcoms.

I'm not expecting anyone and it's only 9 AM, but my doorbell rings and I'm greeted by Tasha, Rylan's sister. We've never officially met, but I saw her when she was in town, and I've seen photos of her so I know what she looks like.

"Bailey? You're Bailey, right?"

"Uhh, yeah?" I respond hesitantly.

"Good, can I come in? Sorry, but this is an emergency." She's pushing past me and my nerves start firing off, my brain starts racing, and I'm frantically trying to piece together what could have happened. My imagination is dark and consists of thousands of true crime stories, so it's always worst case scenario.

"Is he okay?" I ask abruptly, trying to skip the small talk before I spiral.

"No one can get in to see him, he's got himself locked in his room, and I don't know how much you know about his mental health history; but him locking himself away from those that love him, is a recipe for disaster." She's pacing now, also trying not to spiral.

"What can I do to help? We haven't spoken since he walked out over a week ago. He let me know that he was done with me, and I just needed to accept it," I say with my arms crossed over my chest, my eyes fixated on Tasha as she paces my living room.

"God damnit!" She shouts. "Sorry, I'm not upset with you, it's my stupid brother. I know what my family pulled, and I am sorry. That's why I left when I graduated and haven't been back. But Ry, he feels like he owes them."

"I don't know what you expect me to do here?"

"He's in trouble, maybe not like dying in trouble, but he's not just gonna snap out of this on his own. I talked to Cal and Junie, he needs you. Please."

"I-"

"Please," she interrupts before I have a chance to argue. "Cal set up a flight for you and your dog with Rylans pilot, we'll drive you to Denver right now."

I hesitate to agree, but I couldn't bear the thought of something happening to him, and I didn't even make an effort to help. I'm certain he doesn't want to see me, and I'm not even sure I want to see him either. However, Natasha, Cal, and Juniper all believe that I'm the only one who can reach him. So, I have to push my own pain aside to help him him deal with his.

Flying to Dallas alone with Echo was nerve-wracking, but fortunately, Trevor and Stacy, the flight attendants from my first flight with him were there. Stacy even sat with me, keeping me company and making small talk. They're not aware of the situation, but they know Rylan isn't here and can sense that I'm upset about something.

Once we land, Juniper and Cal are waiting for me on the airstrip. Junie rushes over to me and pulls me into a big bear hug, "I'm so glad you're here!" She cries, "We're really worried about him, and I'm sorry we're asking you to do this, despite the pain it may cause you."

"No, it's okay. I understand, and I'm not mad at you for asking."

I allowed Echo to explore the area for a while before Callum got out of the car to retrieve my bag, and offer me a warm embrace before we headed to Rylan's condo. As we drove, they recounted the state of his place, revealing that it was in worse condition than they had initially portrayed. They were hesitant to provide me with the complete picture, recognizing that it would undoubtedly make me feel like I had to come out here, and they wanted to offer me the choice to come, without feeling compelled to.

About twenty minutes later, we reached his building, and Cal hands me the key.

"We'll take Echo back to our place, she can play with our new puppy Roulette, I'm sure they'll have a blast!" Juniper says, reaching for her leash and the backpack with the few belongings that I packed for her. "Yeah, okay. I'm sure she'll love that."

"Please, call me if you need us to come get you, or honestly, just take Ry's keys and car if he keeps himself locked up and you want to get out of there."

"Thanks, I think I'll be okay," I say, with less confidence than I had hoped to exude.

Before I know it, they've driven off with Echo, and I'm taking the elevator up to his floor. His key gripped tightly in my hands, and an overnight bag slung over my shoulder. I look a mess, because let's be honest, I've been doing pretty shit-tastic myself. My hair is in a ponytail, and I threw on my usual go-to outfit of Hey Dudes flats, leggings, and a band t-shirt. This isn't the first time that he's seen me like this, and there's no guarantee he'll even see me now anyways, so I don't really care.

Unlocking the door to his condo, I take a deep breath and push the door open, not entirely sure what to expect. Yes, they gave me details, but nothing could've prepared me for this.

The lights were off, the blinds were drawn completely, and his suitcase sits by the front door, as if he had gotten back from Elk Hollow just today. There's empty plastic water bottles all over his counter, and in his garbage on top there are some takeout containers, banana peels, empty bottles of gatorade and a large empty bottle of vodka. He's not much of a drinker on average, but he's definitely consumed his fair share recently.

I make my way towards the bedroom and knock gently, then attempt to twist the handle, bracing myself for whatever I may see or hear next. It's locked, but he heard me.

"Go. Away. Cal." He shouts sharply through the closed door. "I'm fine, I just need to be alone, don't make me confiscate your key."

"Um, Ry... it's me Bailey." I hear a thud, and some glass bottles clink together. "Think you can let me in?" I back away from the door a little, hoping he'll open it and wanting to give him space.

The door opens slowly, he's disheveled at best and looks like he hasn't showered in days, wearing sweatpants and nothing else. Thankfully he doesn't reek of alcohol; I take that as a good sign.

"What are you doing here, Bailey?" His hand on the door, not letting it open all the way, which lets me know I'm not invited further into his space right now.

"Your friends and family are worried about you, they coordinated a way to get me out here to see if I can help." I take a risk and step closer to him now.

"I told them I'm not what you want, but they said I'm what you *need*. Were they wrong?"

He glances up to meet my gaze, and a fire lights in his eyes, within seconds he's pulling me into his room, into his chest, prying my lips open with his tongue, now thrashing around mine. He's breathing heavily, growling low into my mouth, pulling me deeper into his room, and pushing me lightly onto his bed. I'm getting flashbacks of the last time we were here together and it takes everything in me to stop this.

"Rylan, don't. We can't do this."

"Why?" he snaps, standing in front of me as I sit on the edge of his bed.

"Because we're not together anymore. You told me we were done, and that hurt me, and that meant something to me. I'm not Jessica, I wont sleep with you just because you have money and a dick and are asking for it."

"Get out," He booms loudly, "I need you to leave. Now."

"You don't get to do that Rylan, you don't get to push me away just because you're uncomfortable. You think I wanted to come here, knowing the last time I saw you, you broke my heart and left me to pick up the pieces alone?"

He's still standing there, staring at me blankly before going to pick up a bottle of vodka off the dresser across from the bed, pops open the top, and takes a swig. "Well if you aren't leaving, we're drinking." He says, handing me the bottle now.

"Fine, but you are going to talk to me."

Chapter Twenty-Four

RYLAN

D ay drinking with Bailey was not on my agenda for the day. I was certain that when I left her house, and Elk Hollow, that I would never see her again. Leave it to my baby sister and best friend to force us into close proximity.

She wants answers, and is demanding that I talk to her. I want to drink and get back to wallowing in peace, without having to look her in the eyes and be reminded of the pain I inflicted onto her. We both know who is going to win this battle, and it's not gonna be me. At least she was willing to compromise, and is joining me on the drunk train. Woo Woo.

We've been siting in silence on the floor of my room, passing the bottle back and forth for at least half an hour now. She's let her hair down and is curled up with a blanket, leaning against my bed while I'm sitting with my knees up, across from her. I'm too damn stubborn to say anything first, especially since she's the one that barged in here, and I think she's too scared to make the first move.

Liquor does not make her brave, apparently.

Just as I think that, she clears her throat, "So, why are you such a train wreck? Hmm? You're the one that broke up with me, not the other way around, buddy boy."

Okay, I guess liquor does make her brave, I take that back.

"Who is to say my current state is because of you?" I stagger the words while lackadaisically pointing in her general direction.

"Ha! Obviously it's because of me, I mean look at you. You couldn't keep your hands to yourself when you saw me, and I see the way you're undressing me with your eyes now."

She's not wrong, but I'm not going to admit it.

"I need food, you?" I say standing, well, almost standing. The dresser is holding me up more than my legs are, I think I stood up too fast.

She giggles, "Way to change the subject, boozer."

"I'm not drunk, you are!" I slur, knowing damn well I'm far more drunk than she is. "So how is Tree? Does she hate me?"

"Yes. Yes, she does. Can you blame her? You broke her best friends heart. Juniper isn't very happy with you either."

"Hey! Junie was mine first, back off."

"I'm pretty sure she chose me in the divorce."

"We wouldn't have had to get a divorce if you hadn't gone and fallen in love with me!" I shout faster than I could stop myself. I didn't mean that, I fell in love with her, too.

"Ouch, sorry for getting attached," She rolls her eyes and looks away. I can tell that hurt. Fuck, I did it again, what is my problem?

"If you're really not interested in talking to me, and you really don't have feelings for me anymore,

I'll call your friends and have them pick me up." She goes to stand, and between her general clumsiness and her being drunk, she topples back over and smacks her head on the bedside table.

"Fuck!" She shouts.

"Shit, Bailey," I'm rushing over to her now. "What the fuck are you trying to do, kill yourself and make it look like I murdered you?"

I notice pretty quickly that she has a gash on her temple, it's not very big, but it is bleeding.

"Just stay here, don't move." I say as I head towards the bathroom. Opening every drawer and cabinet, forgetting where I keep things. I finally find the peroxide and bandaids. Next I get a washcloth and q-tip and head back out to the bedroom where she's leaned up again the table she busted her face on.

"Here, let me clean you up. Can you sit up on the bed?"

"I think that's something I could do, maybe." She giggles as I help lift her off the ground and she sits on the edge of the bed.

"You really need to be more careful," I say as I dab the peroxide soaked q-tip to her wound. "I swear one of these days your going to get seriously hurt."

"Not like you care," She snaps back at me and winces.

"Don't be ridiculous, of course I care, Bailey. Why the fuck do you think I left?"

I've finished cleaning her up and placing the bandage over her small cut, and she glances up and meets my gaze.

"You left me. You broke my heart, and left me... because you care? What the fuck kind of logic is that?!" She snaps sarcastically now, tears streaming down her face, and it's not because of the pain from her head.

Instinctively, I reach out and brush her tears away with my thumb, cradling her cheek in the palm of my hand. She leans into it and shudders.

"I trusted you, you made me trust you. You made me feel desired and alive. You treated me like a queen that you worshiped one day, and then the text I was tossed aside like some random hookup, like I was yesterdays trash." She's sobbing now, nothing I say can fix this right now.

I weave my fingers through her hair, and tilt her head, bringing my lips to hers, kissing her deeply, getting lost in her. Pretty soon she is laying on her back, and I'm fumbling with a condom. I know better, I know this isn't what we should be doing, but I'm craving her touch, and I think she's craving mine, too.

I don't stop myself, I don't ask her if it was alright to keep going, I don't think about anything. Once the condom is on and her pants are slid off, I'm sliding in. She's not protesting, but we are both heavily under the influence.

Her body begins writhing underneath mine, arching her back and pushing her pelvis up towards the ceiling.

Calling out my name as she digs her fingernails into my forearms, I can feel her orgasm rushing through her as her muscles tense and the walls of her center tighten and pull me inside further. It's not long before my body starts to quiver and I'm following her into the depths of ecstasy.

Unfortunately, the vodka, coupled with our heightened emotions and the fact that I've been deeply missing her and her body, is not a favorable combination. I'm sloppy and quick, much quicker than I'd ever admit. It's honestly a miracle that my dick is functioning properly in this state.

Once we're cleaned up, exhaustion hits, and we crawl back into bed together. I lie on my back and pull her close to me, inhaling her vanilla strawberry shampoo, and kissing the top of her head.

She rests her head on my chest, with one leg pulled up over mine and her arm wrapped around my stomach. I've missed sleeping next to her, feeling her warmth and the weight of her soft body up against me; comforting me like a weighted blanket. Despite knowing that I'll wake up with a migraine tomorrow morning, this is the best sleep I'll have gotten in weeks.

Scrambling to my feet, slowly and quietly, much quieter than I had anticipated, which saves me the thing that my two kicks fluttering properly in the side.

Rocks were cleared up, exhaustion his, and we spent, but, I flopped together. I lie on my back and pull her close to me, in this heavenly strawberry kitchen until she turns us, off the road.

She collapses, catching her breath with one leg flutted up over mine and her arm wrapped around my stomach. We pressed sleepily, trying to just find the position where he cupped hair was lying ...

"Her ... too ing, that I wake up with her ...
... couple thinks ... this is it, I'm not going to let this ...

Chapter Twenty-Five

BAILEY

I don't know what time it is when I wake up, all I know is that my head is killing me.

It could be from the drinking, or it could be from when I slammed my head into the table beside the bed; either way, I want to die.

Rylan is still passed out, one arm draped across my back, the other tucked under his pillow, and one leg dangling off the side of the bed. He's snoring, and I want to punch him in the face. I'm not typically a violent person, but this morning I could make an exception.

I slip out of the bed as slowly as possible not to wake him, and shuffle my way to the bathroom where I turn the shower on and throw a towel into the warmer. He has some aspirin in the medicine cabinet, and an open bottle of water on the counter I use to toss the pills back. Thank fuck there wasn't vodka in this bottle instead of water.

I don't dare turn the light on, and even though it's relatively dark in here, I can see myself in the mirror and I'm a train wreck. My hair looks like I spent hours on a rollercoaster, and the bags under my eyes are so dark, they could be mistaken for black eyes. I sit for majority of the shower, letting the warm water cascade down my back and It feels incredible.

I see Rylan get up and make his way into the bathroom, and then the shower with me.

"I am not in the mood, keep your penis to yourself."

He chuckles, "Don't worry sunshine, I don't think I have it in me either this morning."

He leaves me to sit under one of the shower heads undisturbed while he washes himself under the other.

It's not long before I'm alone again, staying in one still position until I'm mostly sure that I can get up without vomiting.

Once I'm dried off and dressed, I meet him in the kitchen where he's begun cleaning, and making us breakfast.

The smell quickly makes me feel like I might not be in the clear just yet, but I manage to keep my composure.

"Bacon, eggs, and toast. Trust me, you'll feel better once you eat." He says as he places a plate of food in front of me.

"Sorry about last night, I swear I didn't plan that."

"I don't think any of what happened last night could have been planned, even if we had tried," I say with a smile as I push the eggs around my plate.

"I do want to talk about things though. I know that's what you wanted from me last night, and I'm sorry I couldn't give that to you."

"I'd like to talk about things, too. Just, not until I feel like a human again, and my head is no longer pounding. Deal?"

He chuckles and takes a bite of his toast, "What-ever you say, boozer."

I chuck my crumpled napkin at him, and he lets out a roaring laugh, filling my chest with a warm sensation. I've longed for his laughter, his smile, and just about everything else about him.

The almost two weeks we've spent apart felt like months, and it feels right to be siting here with him again, having breakfast and joking around.

It took a while for me to choke down half of the breakfast that Rylan made for me, but my head is no longer threatening to bring me to jumping off the patio of his high rise loft, and I'm starting to feel like a semi normal person again.

Rylan spent the morning quietly cleaning around me before leaving for a coffee run, and I'm nervous about having to talk to him about things once he returns.

On the one hand, it feels right to be with him again, as if we could effortlessly resume our routine without discussing what happened. On the other hand, he hurt me, and I need to ensure that he won't do it again. I don't know if I can trust him. That is, if he even wants to be with *me* again.

I'm reading when I hear the front door open, followed by a click and the pitter-patter of nails against the wooden floor. I turn around to see Echo sprinting through the living room towards me. She leaps onto the couch and immediately lunges for my face.

"I missed my girl. I had to rescue her from Cal and Junie before they got too attached and refuse to give her back."

"Your girl?" As if she could hear me, she abruptly leaps off the couch and surges towards him, jumping on him and licking his hands frantically, desperately striving to get as close to him as possible. What a traitor!

"Dogs choose their people, you can't fault me for that." He says while petting her head and leaning down to give her kisses on her snout.

We continue to beat around the bush for he next hour; playing with Echo, engaging in superficial conversation, and sipping our coffees that I actually asked for. I needed something a little stronger than tea today.

I'm curled up on the couch, resting my back against the armrest, with my knees bent and legs folded into each other as I twirl my fingers around a loose thread in the knit blanket that's resting in my lap.

"So uh, I'm sorry about how I handled things," He says, running his hands through his hair, glancing down at me from the kitchen bar stool he's sitting at.

"Last night, or two weeks ago?"

"Both? All of the above? I mean, you weren't exactly complaining last night," He wriggles his eyebrows at me and grins.

"Of course, I mean all of it."

He stands and joins me on the couch, pulling my legs out and lifting them to spread across his lap. He begins rubbing my feet over my socks, and damn it feels amazing.

"So what do we do now?" I ask, hesitant to get an answer I don't want to hear. Please say you want to get back together, please tell me you love me back.

"Well, I think I need to figure shit out with my family and the business. It's toxic, and so are they.

I want out, and I think in order for me to move forward with my life, I need to handle that shit first."

That's not exactly what I was hoping to hear, but I know he's right. I begin to pull my legs back into myself, but he holds firm and prevents me from doing so.

"That doesn't mean that I want to lose you again." He says in a low and firm tone, he almost sounds angry now.

"I don't know how you can have both right now."

"We take it slow, but you're mine."

"I'm yours?" I ask with a soft voice, tilting my head searching for confirmation.

"You're mine."

Chapter Twenty-Six

RYLAN

I'm fully aware that I should get my shit together before committing to Bailey again, especially since there seems to be more of a spoken commitment between us now than there was before.

The idea of losing her again tears me up though, and I can't have that. I can't let her slip through my fingers again.

I've never addressed her as mine aloud before yesterday. In fact, I've never called anyone mine prior to yesterday. However, she *is* mine, and always will be if I have the final say.

I will give her the world, and never let her feel like she's not worthy of every bit of it.

She's hesitant and cautious, which is understandable. I know she'll need time to fully embrace our relationship again, but she's giving me this chance, which I know is far more than I deserve.

Bailey has to return to Colorado tomorrow. She's missed too much work, and Violet has been incredibly accommodating these past few weeks, allowing Bailey to fly back and forth for various reasons.

I'm not looking forward to telling her, even though I think a part of her knows this needs to happen, but I can't go back with her. I need to stay and take care of things. If I want to have any chance of creating a future with Bailey, I need to put this life behind me, but that's going to take a little bit of time.

What she doesn't know is that I've already researched buying land just outside of Elk Hollow. I've been particularly interested in two lots and have already drawn up blueprints for my vision with Callum. It's going to be perfect once completed. A cozy cabin with a wrap-around porch, and a large shop barn that can also serve as a guest apartment.

I've assembled the necessary team and have the finances in place. Only piece that's missing is taking the plunge. I had begun planning this prior to our breakup, but the past few weeks have stalled the progress.

Aside from creating a space for Bailey and I to grow in, I'm most excited about the shop that I'm building next to the cabin. Woodworking has always been a skill that I've possessed. I took shop in high school and still have some of the pieces that I completed, including a blanket chest that I'm planning to give to Bailey. She saw it her first weekend here and fell in love with it, stating she'd never seen anything more beautiful.

I'm happiest when I'm working with my hands, and I can see myself making a living doing it even though I've never crafted anything to sell. I just need to finish cutting ties with everything here, as difficult as it will be.

Thankfully, money isn't an issue or a factor. Whatever money I have in the bank is mine to keep, and I'm overall pretty careful with spending and investing. I could afford to live comfortably for the rest of my life with what I have, even if I don't make anymore.

"I'll be back soon," I say reassuringly as I wrap my arms around Bailey, not wanting to say goodbye on the airstrip.

"You better," she says, gripping me tightly and looking up at me, inviting me in for a kiss.

I can tell she's sad about leaving without me. I don't feel great about it either considering we haven't been together in weeks, and just as we fix things between us, we're being pulled apart again.

After they board, I sit in my car and watch them take off, wishing I was up there with them.

Now, the real work can begin though. I have a meeting with a realtor scheduled for later today, as well as interviews with a few different moving companies. I'll require temporary storage for most of my belongings, and once I'm ready, the moving company will need to collect them from the storage unit and then transport them to Colorado for me.

Callum offered to come over and help me organize some things before my meeting with my lawyer later this week. I can't confront my father until my affairs are in order, and I want to ensure there are no loose ends. Additionally, Cal believes his brother might be interested in purchasing my place, which could potentially speed up the selling process. I'll also need to sell my car, but thankfully that should be the easiest transaction.

Pulling up to my building's parking garage, all I can think about is wrapping things up as quickly as possible, and beginning the process on the cabin while I'm still here so things are underway.

I'm desperate to be back to Colorado. It's crazy how much I couldn't wait to get back home when I first left, but Elk Hollow is more home to me than Dallas ever was. Especially with Bailey being there.

It's been a few weeks and I can finally say I'm almost finished with what I need to handle out here. Thank fuck for that because I am really missing Bailey.

I miss the smell of her hair, the feel of her soft body pushed up against mine while we cuddle in bed, and I miss her laugh. The one where when she really gets going, it's a silent laugh that makes me question if she's even breathing, and sometimes she slaps her leg like she had heard the funniest joke ever to be told. I still remember the first time she did it, she was so corny and said "that was a real knee slapper, eh?" God she's adorable.

She hasn't answered most of my texts, and none of my calls recently. She mentioned something about having a stomach bug and has called out sick from work the past few days. I offered to fly back early, but she basically told me to fuck off and that she doesn't need no man. Which I am very well aware of, but it would be nice if she was more open to me being there for her. We've had endless discussions about her doubts and concerns since our fight and my walking out.

While it will be liberating to see the rest of my plans through, I'm not particularly excited about it.

Initially, I planned to wait until my brother took over the company to separate from it, but if I want to regain Bailey's trust and move forward with my life, I need to severe the ties completely.

My family has caused enough damage, and what transpired with them here last month was the final straw.

Chapter Twenty-Seven

BAILEY

Two lines?! I frantically reach for the box and flail it every which way in a panic to see what two lines indicate. What. The. Fuck. Suddenly I feel extremely faint, the room is dark, and I can't breathe. This cannot be happening.

Thankfully, Aspen isn't home right now, so this revelation is between me and the four walls of this bathroom, and may they speak now or forever hold their peace. I don't really know what I was expecting, it's not like I've been celibate and I'm not on birth control.

I've never needed to be on it until I met Rylan and things took off so fast, I didn't even have time to think about it. Especially since we've been using condoms. I know they can break, but we never noticed it happening. Still, for some unknown reason his little spermies decided to take hostage in my uterus, and it's a little too late to think about birth control now.

I suppose the primary reason I didn't consider my period being late was because I attributed it to the stress and pain I'd been experiencing regarding things with Rylan since everything escalated. My emotions were all over the place for a few weeks, and I couldn't regulate anything in my life, why would I have expected my menstrual cycle to be regulated either.

I sit on the side of the tub for the better part of the next hour contemplating just how the fuck I plan to handle this, and wonder how long I can get away without showing signs of being with child. I shudder at the thought. It's not like babies gross me out or anything, or like I never want to be a mother. But right now? With Rylan? Okay.. maybe with Rylan. His babies would be beautiful, and he can afford to support a baby that's for sure. But would he want to have a baby with me? Does he even want to have a baby at all? The conversation has never come up.

How am I even going to tell him? We don't exactly have the kind of relationship right now that would prompt a cute little surprise moment people capture on camera and post to TikTok. I can't put my pee stick in a box with a onesie that says "Little Bean Brewing! New Blend Coming 2024!" with a picture of a baby sized coffee mug.

Oh, I'm gonna hurl. Honestly, I can't tell if it's the tenant I've got taking up real-estate inside of my womb, or my spiraling thoughts that is causing my sudden onset bout of nausea. Whatever is, is now the reason I am becoming one with the inside of the porcelain throne. At least I manic cleaned the bathroom last night instead of sleeping.

Missed Calls : 3
Unread Text Messages : 7
Times I've Puked : I've Lost Count

I've come to terms with my newfound illness, and decided to make my life easier by creating a bed in the bathtub so I'm right next to the toilet. It's been three days, and I am without a doubt suffering from morning sickness. I still haven't figured out why they call it morning sickness though. It's not just in the morning. Must've been a term coined by a man, but I digress. I've had to call out every single day this week, and Aspen has been staying with her boyfriend, Micah.

She's afraid of catching whatever I have, and it took everything in me not to say if she wants to avoid what I have, then she should not be sleeping over at Micah's more frequently.

I know I need to get in to see an OBGYN, but the closest one is down the mountain 40 minutes away, and I really hate doctors. I won't go to the local clinic because it's a small town that doesn't even have a OBGYN, plus word gets around here fast.

All I ever hear is that I'm obese and anything wrong with me is due to that. I've sworn off doctors for the past few years. Women used to have babies by themselves all the time so why couldn't I? I'd consider this further if my main concern wasn't getting a prescription filled for this "morning" sickness, so I can go back to work sooner rather than later. On the plus side, I'll probably shed a few pounds with all this puking.

Rylan has been back in Dallas for the past two weeks, which makes dodging him rather easy. I responded to one of his messages yesterday, but none of his phone calls or new texts. We've been easing back into things as he's working on himself and getting things in order back home.

Ry is a good man, and would make an excellent partner and provider. But would he make a good dad, or would he be too jaded from his father?

I've already decided that shortly after he returns, I'm going to tell him about the pregnancy. This isn't something that should be done over text, even I can see how fucked that is. Especially considering that while he's in Dallas taking care of things at the office, he's planning on meeting with his family and cutting ties with them temporarily.

We are just barely finding ourselves again, and I can't put this on him right now on top of everything else.

Family is such a tough subject, and I'm not sure he's ready to hear that I'm adding to it.

Chapter Twenty-Eight

RYLAN

I sent a group text to my family, excluding Tash, and instructed them to meet me at the house tonight at 5 pm. As I ascended the long steps, my chest tightened, and every instinct within me urged me to turn back. However, my heart compelled me to proceed. I need to confront them and ultimately sever ties with them if I want to have any chance of moving forward in my life.

I refrain from knocking, I can see that everyone is already here and waiting for me. I'm usually early, but my anxiety coupled with the feeling of wanting to stick it to them, made me late by fifteen minutes.

Once inside, my mother stands to great me with a hug, "Oh Rylan, I'm so glad you're home again," she says with a smile.

Kyle nods, Rachel gently bounces her youngest child in her lap, and her husband, Daniel, guides the two older children into the kitchen for a snack.

My father, Adam, remains motionless and doesn't even glance my way. It's only when I'm seated at the opposite end of the table that he finally lifts his gaze to meet mine.

"Rylan," he says in a cold tone. "Have you come to your senses?"

"I have. I'm leaving the company. And after today, I will be needing to take space apart from this family. I've finished clearing out my condo, and I'll be moving back to Elk Hollow full time from here on out." I state as firmly and calmly as possible, keeping emotion to a minimum.

"Don't be ridiculous," Kyle snaps. "This isn't because of that girl, is it?"

"Actually Kyle, it's because I'm sick and tired of the way this family treats each other and outsiders, and the fucked up views this family has on the world. But also, yes, it's because of *that* girl, whose name is Bailey. She is kind, beautiful, and wonderful, and she accepts me for me, and not who I'm expected to be." Standing now, my eyes moving from Kyles to our fathers.

"She could, and *should* have fled from me forever the moment that she met you all and endured what you subjected her to. But she chose to stay by my side. I was the one who fled, the one who pushed her away when it was all of *you* that I should have cast aside instead. I'm going to marry that girl one day, and she will be all the family that I need." I say with finality, making my way to the tables end, stopping beside my father who is still sitting in silence.

"My lawyer has everything you'll need and will be in touch, Adam."

No one says anything, but I can see tears forming in my mothers eyes. She begins to reach out for my arm, but my father clears his throat to get her attention and nods in disapproval.

With that, I walk out of the Sterling home with no intention on coming back any time soon or ever.

Finally, I'm back where I belong. That was the longest three weeks between meeting with the family, taking care of things at the office with my lawyer, and packing up my condo.

It's September now, the leaves have almost completed their change, and there's a crisp chill in the air. I'm ready to fall back into my new normal here before the holidays roll around, starting with Bailey and Echo.

She's stubborn as hell, and I haven't heard anything from her since she told me I didn't need to fly back early to take care of her. I called her again on my drive up from Denver and she sent me to voicemail.

I would be worried that she's pulling away out of fear I will abandon her again, except I reached out to Aspen who told me she was busy covering extra shifts.

I can appreciate her determination to provide for herself, she's extremely independent and I love that about her, but once I make her mine officially, she will need to learn how to lean on me for things as well. I refuse to let her carry all the burdens and responsibilities.

Just because she doesn't require more than the bare minimum, doesn't mean that's what my girl deserves.

Pulling up into the duplex parking lot makes me feel like I can finally breathe again. I figured I'd unload the truck, head up for a quick shower, and wait here until Bailey is home to give her the chest and see how she's feeling.

I've missed her like crazy, and not being able to talk to her while I've been gone was brutal.

Chapter Twenty-Nine

RYLAN

B ailey had gotten home while I was in the shower and sent a text letting me know that she was going to head over soon. I spent the time waiting for her unpacking my bags that had some toys I bought for Echo, as well a set of wooden bookends for Bailey that I carved and painted in Callum's shop. I had some downtime to create and I wanted to design something special for her while I was in between responsibilities.

When I open the door to greet her, I have the urge to close the space between us and press my lips to hers, but I can tell her energy is off.

"Hey Bailey Boo, I've missed you. Are you feeling better?" She shoots a quick half-smile and slides past me, avoiding my embrace which is not what I had expected.

"Work has been stressful since one of the girls at the bar quit and left Micah hanging. Aspen took her shifts, so I've been down a body in the coffee shop for the past week." She says as she goes to sit on the couch and places a pillow in front of her stomach to hide behind.

"Damn, I'm sorry to hear that, no wonder I haven't heard from you." I say as I go to join her on the couch. She's in the corner seat of the sectional, her favorite spot, with her legs stretched out facing the door. I bring her feet up into my lap and she doesn't pull her legs away so I take that as a good sign.

"I have a few interviews lined up for tomorrow, I'll hire just about anyone at this point," she sighs, "I am exhausted."

"Is there anything that I can do?" I'm sure she'll say no even if there was something that I can do to help.

"Actually, I think you can-" She trails off and I'm really curious to see where this conversation goes.

"Can you find a buyer for the shop? I know you have connections and that you're in the business of investing in property."

As much as I know she thinks she wants me to do this, it wouldn't be beneficial to anyone if I did. Of course she finally asks for my help, and it's the one thing I can't make happen for her.

"Is Violet thinking of selling now? I know she mentioned it a while back, but I thought she agreed to wait for Aspen to be take over?"

"Aspen isn't going to take over, that's the thing. We thought by giving her time to acclimate to the idea, that she would change her mind and be ready. But she wants to leave the management positions up to Micah and someone else."

"Let me meet with Violet and I'll see what we can do, but I can't make any promises. I hope you understand."

Leaning back into the pillow she's placed behind herself now, she lets out a sigh and tells me she's appreciates my agreeing to meet with Vy even if that's all that happens.

"I have something for you," I say as I go to stand. I've placed the toys and bookends into the chest that is hidden behind the kitchen counter.

"Let me get it." Her eyes widen as she sits herself up a little higher in anticipation.

I'm rounding the corner when she caught a glimpse of the chest in my hands, and shouts my name. "Rylan!" Her hands covering her face. "You brought me the chest!" She exclaims.

"I know how much you love it, and I thought it would look perfect in your room. Open it up."

She sifts through the dog toys and comes up on the bookends. "Ry. These... Are beautiful. Where did you get them?"

Tears falling from her face now. I knew she would like them, but I think I underestimated just how much. I haven't told her that I made the chest yet, or that I make anything for that matter. But I want her to know how much she means to me, and how special giving these to her is.

"I made them for you when I was in Dallas. I also made the blanket chest."

Blinking and not saying a word, she begins to sob now. She stands to give me a hug, and I hold her there until she pulls away. This is the Bailey I had been missing, this is the Bailey I had been expecting to see once I got back home.

I've been a back for a few weeks now, and I can see that something is still bothering Bailey. I know it isn't just the coffee shop because she was able to hire someone to fill Aspens shifts which lessoned her workload.

She hasn't come out and said something else was wrong, but I can feel it. So much so that I asked Aspen about it when I ran into her last night. She didn't know what I was talking about, however she admitted that she hasn't seen much of her lately with them having opposite schedules now.

Bailey told me she didn't need me to meet with Violet about Brews N Booze anymore, Vy's sister wants to buy her out, which puts me at ease. I still haven't had the chance to tell her that I resigned from S&S and no longer have the connections required to help Violet out, aside from giving her advice anyways.

Another thing I haven't shared with her yet is that I've bought the land where I'll be building the cabin, and I've also placed the order for the lumber. The lot clearing began last week, so we can start construction immediately.

I paid top dollar for the materials, this is the home that I want us to grow old together in. I need it to be constructed to last for multiple generations and families.

I understand that winter is approaching rapidly, but I was hoping that if we began preparing in advance, I could have it ready before next winter. I have no doubt that we will reach my end date goal for the cabin, and maybe even be able to move into the shop barn with the apartment loft long before then.

I fully recognize that I shouldn't keep her in the dark about these changes, but when I mentioned ending my relationship with my family temporarily, I believe she took on the responsibility for that decision. I attempted to convince her that our relationship has always been this challenging, and that she was the catalyst I needed to move forward.

Lately, she seems extra fragile, as if she's on the verge of breaking if something more happens. I'm not sure if it's due to what's happening with my family, our relationship, or both. But I do know that I need to be more careful with her and give her the space and time she needs to feel comfortable with me again.

I will give her all the time and space that she needs, because she's worth it.

Chapter Thirty

BAILEY

I know that I need to tell Rylan about the pregnancy, I had planned on doing it the day he came back. But hell, I just couldn't. He surprised me with gifts for Echo and I, as well as the blanket chest I obsessed over. I stood there crying in his arms, knowing damn well the fetus inside me played a huge part in why I was overly emotional. But it felt weird to be like "Hey, thanks for the gifts. I got a gift for you, too! A baby, surprise!" Yeah, no.

Something is drawing me closer to him, though. I'm more addicted to the feeling that he gives me when I can see him, feel his touch, or even smell him for fucks sake. It's almost animalistic. I was keeping my distance from him emotionally for obvious reasons at first, but physically all I've wanted is to jump his bones every time I see him.

I wonder if this is pregnancy hormones or just because I missed him so much when he broke things off and then left for Dallas.

I know it isn't logical, but now that his first day back since I've found out about the baby has long since passed, I feel like I've missed my opportunity and it would be fucked up to drop this on him after hiding it for a few months now. The more time that passes, the more I begin to freak out over telling him.

The prescription meds for my nausea have been helping overall, but I still throw up if I move too quickly, or if I don't lightly snack throughout the day or drink enough water. I've managed to hide every time I've been sick up until last week when we went to the diner for a date.

The smells were fine at first, and I thought I was safe with ordering a side of french fries, and salad without meat, since meat had been giving me issues lately. Rylan ordered chicken fried steak though, and as soon as it was brought to our table and placed in front of me, I almost tossed my cookies all over his plate. Thankfully I was able to choke it down long enough to sprint to the bathroom.

When I returned to the table, he knew what I had gotten up to do and was concerned that I might have the stomach flu again. He requested that I make a doctors appointment if I was still feeling off in the morning.

Aspen has essentially moved in with Micah permanently. It's not because there's anything amiss between us; it's simply more convenient for them to carpool to work now. While I miss her, I'm grateful that we still have our weekly movie nights, which are the only nights she stays over now.

She still pays rent, but we're considering finding a more affordable arrangement for both of us. There's no reason for her to continue paying rent for a place she rarely uses. Moreover, Micah and Aspen have been dating for several years now, and this move would be a natural progression in their relationship.

My most recent OBGYN appointment was last week, and I measured around 15 weeks, almost halfway there. I'm not showing yet, in part because I'm only in the beginning of my second trimester, but also because I'm overweight. Even though I lost about 10 pounds during my first trimester with how often I was sick, I'm still a thick girl and it didn't really change my appearance.

Rylan and I have been increasingly sexually active lately, I think my sex drive is through the roof due to my pregnancy, but I'm worried he'll notice changes in my body sooner than later. I'm just thankful he hasn't asked why I haven't appeared to have a period recently which would normally affect when we have intercourse. And thankfully I'm not a big drinker, which has been my saving grace and he hasn't questioned why I've turned down wine with dinner.

I know that with my twenty week appointment scheduled in a few weeks, I'll be able to see the gender if I want to, and I also opted for the amniocentesis to check for any of the main developmental abnormalities.

I'm feeling anxious about this upcoming appointment, even more so than the initial one to confirm the accuracy of the six sticks I peed on. I've attended every appointment alone so far, as I still haven't shared the news with anyone yet. However, I genuinely want Rylan to be there for this visit.

My connection with Rylan isn't the only one that's been strengthening lately. My bond with this baby is far deeper than I ever anticipated. I often find myself placing my hand on my stomach whenever

I'm alone. Additionally, I read, talk, and sing to it often. And I think Echo knows someone is in there, as her favorite place to lay her head now is my stomach.

I haven't bought anything for the baby yet, or even thought about names. I think a part of me is disconnected because there's a missing link right now. It would be one thing if the father knew and wasn't a part of things voluntarily, it's another that he doesn't know and yet is always around.

I'm finding it hard to plan or get excited, and I know I'm the only one holding me back from moving forward.

Christmas and the New Year have come and gone, and I managed to see my family without them suspecting a thing. I felt awful leaving Rylan behind, knowing he wasn't going back to Dallas to be with his family for the Holidays, but he promised me that everything was okay, and that he would see me New Years day when I got back from my parents.

I have my twenty week ultrasound appointment on Monday, and I've decided I don't want to do this without Rylan anymore. This gives me three days to tell him, and I've officially made a plan to do it tonight during dinner once he's off of work.

I'm going to ease him into it, ask questions that will hint at my being pregnant, and see how he responds. I have no idea what to expect as our relationship doesn't even have a label right now, and we haven't exactly been having future plans conversations outside of him wanting to leave the family business to pursue woodworking, which I fully support and admire. He is amazing with his hands and I see the amount of joy it brings him. We also discussed my potential plans for wanting to own my own coffee shop someday, which he is also extremely supportive of, and doesn't appear to have any doubts in my abilities to make that dream my reality whenever I'm ready.

That's about as far as we've gotten with talking about the future though, so I'm walking in completely blind.

It's Friday and Aspen left for Micah's a few hours ago to spend the weekend with him. I know we'll have the place to ourselves so this time I invited him to have dinner over here. I had the day off so I spent the morning cleaning, and now I'm heading into town to get a few things from the grocery store.

We don't have everything a big box store would have, but we have minimal options of just about everything a full sized grocery store would carry, thankfully.

Aimlessly wandering up and down the aisles with a small cart, I find myself in the baby section. There are diapers, formula, bottles, and pacifiers. But there are also a few sets of baby clothes in various sizes. We have a few small clothing shops in the next town over, and someone local is always selling or giving away kids' items. However, I haven't even considered any of that. But thinking about telling Rylan about the baby, our baby, I feel a sudden urge to buy something. I quickly glance around and grab the first thing that catches my eye. It's a onesie that says, "I love My Daddy."

For dinner I plan to make my favorite, it's something I know baby, and subsequently I, can stomach eating. Vegetarian enchiladas with black olives on top. I make my way around the store, gathering all the ingredients as well as a bag of lettuce for a side salad.

When I make it to the front of the store to checkout, I round the corner and bump into Aspen. "Shit! Oh my God, Sorry Bailey!"

"Oh hey, it's alright," I say as I bounce between eyeing the baby paraphernalia sitting in my cart, and then back to Aspen. Trying to will her into not looking, but also unintentionally drawing her eyes to figure out what I'm looking at.

"You know how clumsy I am, totally my fault for not taking the corner slower!"

"Oo- what's this?" She pulls the baby onesie out of the basket and holds it up while reading aloud. "Aww, who is this for?"

Bringing the onesie down to look at me, almost as if she can read it on my face she immediately drops it back into the cart and throws her arms around me.

"Oh my God! Why haven't you told me? I should've known you didn't have a stomach bug a few months ago."

Standing in the middle of the aisle, hugging Aspen, I begin to cry. It feels so amazing to know I'm not alone in this journey anymore, and suddenly I wish I had told her so much sooner. I know I could have, she would've been supportive and probably gone to every appointment with me even if I didn't ask her to.

"I'm so sorry I didn't tell you. I think I was just scared," I say as I let go to wipe the tears from my face with my hoodie sleeve. "Rylan doesn't know yet either, you're actually the first person to find out."

"Bailey! Is there anything I can do for you? When are you planning on telling him?" She blurted loudly, unaware of her lack of indoor voice. "Soon, actually. That's why I bought the onesie."

Aspen gives me another hug and lets me know that if I need anything at all, she's right there, Micah and the bar be damned. I appreciate her, and I would be lying if I said I wasn't missing her like crazy. Especially since I've been going through this pregnancy without my best friend. Again, only I'm to blame for that.

She also promised that she wouldn't tell anyone except Micah if I was alright with that, which of course I was as long as he promised not to say anything either. The worst thing that could happen is small town talk getting back to Rylan before I have a chance to tell him myself. I shudder at the thought.

Chapter Thirty-One

RYLAN

I'm feeling almost giddy about my date with Bailey tonight. Her sex drive has been off the charts lately, and she's been more open to getting closer to me emotionally without much resistance.

Additionally, we've made significant progress on the lot since I began to focus on renovating my house full-time. Tonight, I'm finally going to show her the blueprints and photos of what we've accomplished so far.

We began with the shop barn, which also serves as a loft apartment. This arrangement allows me to move into the apartment and have a workspace while I await the completion of the rest of the property.

The barn is approximately 75% finished right now, and I have already started purchasing paint and furniture for the apartment which I'm really fuckin excited about. I don't think I've ever been as excited about a project as I am with this one, and I know it's because of what it represents and who I'll be sharing it with.

I understand that Aspen has been living with Micah, and the girls are contemplating breaking the lease for the duplex to save money. Because of that, I'm optimistic that presenting these plans to Bailey now will persuade her to move into the loft with me. Especially since things with us have been going back to normal.

The apartment loft might not be as big as my condo was or the duplexes are, but it offers a bedroom, a fully equipped kitchen with a breakfast nook, a master bathroom complete with a walk-in closet and a tub for her relaxing marathon baths. Also a living room, and a reading nook with floor-to-ceiling bookcases in the corner by a window. This living space should accommodate us and Echo for the year it may take to renovate the cabin and the surrounding areas. I have meticulously designed almost every aspect of the loft with them in mind.

I've been feeling guilty about concealing my activities from her. She still believes I'm at the job site in town every day. I haven't been intentionally lying; I've been at a job site, just not the one she's thinking of.

I've decided to come clean tonight, about the construction and my being currently unemployed.

Stepping through the unlocked front door of Bailey's house, I can smell something burning and can hear her coughing.

I look to my right to see her fanning some oven mitts around a baking dish that's sitting haphazardly on he edge of the stovetop. Cooking isn't necessarily her strong suit, but everything she's made for me up to this point has been edible.

I'm not so sure about what's happening here though.

"What happened, did the oven dragon not like the food?" I say with a laugh. Startled and up to this point completely unaware of my presence, she stops fanning to glance up at me.

"I fell asleep on the couch. And now it's all ruined!" I can see that her emotions are at an all time high.

"It's okay sweetheart. It's just-" I can't finish the sentence before she barks back,

"It's not okay, and it's not just food!"

Woof, okay. Looks like I need to do some serious damage control. This is not how I pictured this evening going but I'm up for the challenge.

"Did you start your period?" I ask, knowing how dangerous of a question that was, but I had a point to why I was asking.

She scoffs, "No, not like it's any of your business though. Are you saying that I'm being overly emotional and irrational? Because if so-"

Now it's my turn to interrupt her. She's cute when she's feisty.

I make my way towards her, pulling the oven mitts out of her hands and backing her up into the wall. I twist my fingers into her hair and lightly pull her head up to look at me. As I brush the back of my other hand across her cheek, I lean down to whisper into her ear, "I don't need to eat dinner tonight, not while I have you in front of me." Her knees buckle as I press into her, peppering kisses on her neck and shoulder that's exposed by her loose sweater.

She brings her knee up into my crotch and rubs it up and down over my cock. I let out a hiss.

I was hard before she started rubbing against me, now I'm really primed and ready to devour her. I guide her to the bedroom and walk her backwards into the foot of the bed and demand she sit down.

Once she's situated I slide her to the edge of the bed, and strip her of her leggings and underwear.

Running my fingers across her eager pussy, she's soaked and just the lightest touch makes her moan and arch her back towards the ceiling. I spread her legs and bring my tongue to her slit, God she tastes so fucking good. She tastes better than she ever has before.

She's grinding on my mouth, moving in circular motions and pulling on my hair with one hand while the other is up by her head. She's frantic and needful, begging for more. I lap at her clit and push three fingers inside her forcefully.

"I need your cock, Ry," She says breathlessly. "Please."

"Fuck baby, let me get a condom. Hold on," I go to stand so I can retrieve one stashed in her nightstand.

"No!" She shouts before I can get off the floor. "It's not necessary, we're covered. Please, let me feel you come inside of me."

I let out a growl and have my pants off faster than I've ever undressed before. She must've started birth control, thank fuck because I know she is going to feel like amazing. It probably won't take me very long to finish, but I plan to make every fucking second of this count.

"Fuck baby," I say as I lift her leg and rub the tip of my cock up and down her pussy.

"You're going to feel so good. Are you sure this is what you want?"

She reaches around her thigh and digs her nails into my forearm. "Please, Ry."

That was all the permission I needed. With that, I slam into her, going as deep as her our bodies would allow and bottoming out.

Fuck she's so tight and wet. I've never gone bare before and this is the most amazing feeling my dick has ever experienced.

I'm addicted and I will never be able to go back to using condoms. I will never be able to have another pussy again either.

It's not long before we reach our climax, she wanted me to pound into her as fast and as hard as possible. She was desperate to orgasm as quickly as I could make her.

Normally I would protest, but I could tell she needed things to be a specific way tonight, so despite my dick feeling like it was being consumed by pure heaven, I obliged.

"I'm going to come, Ry," She shouts in between moans. "Come with me."

"Fuck baby, that's it," I suck in a breath, slam into her as deep as I can, and pinch her clit.

Her body begins to writhe underneath mine, she's groaning and gripping at the pillow underneath her pelvis. I can feel her tighten as she releases. I can't hold back and my cock pulses and thickens inside of her. Goddamn I could stay right here forever.

We lay there together for a few minutes before I stand to turn on the shower.

"Here baby, why don't you clean up while I make us something to eat." I hand her the robe from the bathroom and pull my jeans back on, then kiss the top of her head before heading to the kitchen.

I wanted to stay in bed with her and cuddle until morning, but I know we needed to eat something and talk about things first. We will have the rest of our lives to spend together.

Chapter Thirty-Two

BAILEY

O nce I was finished showering, I came out to the living room to find Rylan with a plate of buttered noodles and the side salad that I had grabbed for the enchiladas. He hasn't touched his plate and waits until I'm seated next to him at the table to eat.

I'm not sure if it was from the workout in the form of sex, or the baby, but I was feeling insatiable. I scarfed my serving down incredibly fast and went back for seconds. I was too hungry to care what he may think of my current eating habits, but he didn't mention it or give me a look of disgust or disproval.

His dark brown is disheveled, and he's wearing jeans and a grey form fitting t-shirt. I want to reach across the table and run my fingers through his hair. Just as I go to act on my desires, he stands and carries our dishes to the sink. God, a man that cooks and cleans, *he's perfect* I think to myself as I watch him take care of the dishes from my mess and his.

I know I still need to talk to him about what's going on in my uterus and Monday morning, but again I can feel myself chickening out. I just need to start off slow.

"Hey, so um-" I trail off and wait for him to look up from the casserole dish I defiled with my fire hazard,

"What do you think about kids?" I ask nonchalantly.

"Kids? They are alright. My nieces and nephew are okay. I haven't spent much time around them though, and I think they have a childhood far too similar to mine." He's resumed the dishes now and I can tell he wants to say something else so I nudge a little more.

"Care to elaborate a little for me?" I say now moving to sit at the bar on the opposite side of the sink where he stands.

"Well, I guess I just don't appreciate how things were done, and are being done in my family. Especially when it comes to raising children. It's fucked and all we're doing is pumping out little worker bees to make the Sterlings more wealthy. That was too much pressure on us, and now on them. My sister Rachel is barely functioning and Kyle," He sighs. "I'm not even sure he's going to ever fucking change. The worst thing the Sterlings could do is continue to populate."

And with that comment, I have lost all desire and confidence to let him know about what's going on with me. Honestly, as much as I don't personally believe I could ever go through with an abortion, I think I might have considered it if we had had this conversation earlier on. But now I'm too far along, and my heart is far too attached to this tiny human that I'm growing inside of me.

"On that note though," He says, pausing to look back up at me from the dishes. "When I was back home, I didn't just leave my family. I left it all. The company, the condo, everything."

Excuse me, what? My mind is racing, and I can't seem to find the right words. I'm happy for him, but I also can't understand why he kept these things from me. Fuck, Bailey, what are you even saying? He's not the only one holding onto a pretty deep fucking secret, here.

I join him in the kitchen, and silently wrap my arms around him, giving him a tight hug. We remain there for a few moments, neither of us commenting on what he said or continuing the baby conversation.

Despite this, the rest of the evening runs smoothly. We watch a movie, take Echo out for a quick walk, and then return to the bedroom for another quick session before falling asleep with his arms wrapped around me. I believe it was better for both of us to pretend that nothing happened or was said.

Saturday morning I can feel his chest rising and falling against my back, and his warm breath on my neck. He has one arm under the pillow, supporting my head, and the other resting across my side, just under my breasts. The orange glow of the sun rising threatens to peek through the cracks between the curtain panels over my window.

Rylan had gifted me something, something bigger than anything I had ever received before.

This secret I'm hiding from him could shatter our relationship once he discovers the truth, and I fear I might lose him, forever this time. I might even have to raise this child on my own and that terrifies me.

It's Monday morning, and I find myself alone in the waiting room of the OBGYN's. During my drive here, I called Aspen to inform her of my appointment, and arrange to meet her at the coffee shop afterward.

She's incredibly excited and has already affectionately begun calling herself Auntie Aspen. This adorable gesture fills me with hope that I won't be entirely alone during this time. While I know my parents would be supportive, I'm reluctant to relocate back to Denver, and they're unwilling to move up here either. I know that's me jumping to worst case scenario, and I have what, twenty weeks give or take to figure it out. I'm not able to dwell on this much longer before my thoughts are interrupted.

"Bailey Collins?" My name is called out by a pretty brunette in pink scrubs standing in the doorway. She has a flashy smile and kind eyes, the type of person you can feel safe with during at a time like this, which I appreciate.

"Alright, Mama. Are you ready to see your baby?" Mama, that's the first time I've been called that. I feel a flutter in my stomach and a smile sweeps across my face.

"Yes, so ready."

She takes a series of photos for me, and asks if I'd like to know the gender. I decline and she makes a note in my chart to let everyone else know not to say anything.

Now it's time for my amniocentesis, and for this procedure I'm moved into a different exam room.

The doctor comes in and records some things, they take some blood, and then begin to go over the procedure with me.

I'm a little nervous, but she assures me there are very rarely complications, and with my family history and how the baby is looking on the scans, she doesn't expect any big surprises.

A flash of something, I'm not sure if it's intuition or fear comes over me when she mentions the risks and lets me know that this procedure is most likely not even necessary considering how everything has been looking up to this point. I almost tell her to stop and just run the simple blood tests, but I want to ensure everything is okay with my baby, so I don't interfere despite the nagging feeling.

I don't remember the test being done, and I vaguely remember begging them to call Rylan Sterling from my phone, then I'm out again.

I also don't remember being awake for anything else or know long I was out. But when I do wake up, Rylan is sleeping in a chair pulled up next to my bed. His arm draped across my lap and head resting on my stomach.

I look to my left and see my mother sleeping on a cot, and my father in a recliner under a big window. It's dark outside, but bright in the hallway. It's disorienting and my eyes begin to feel heavy again. I drift off to sleep before I have time to think about where I'm at, why they are here, or if me and the baby are alright.

Chapter Thirty-Three

RYLAN

We hadn't gotten any snow over the weekend and it's surprisingly really warm out today, so I'm up at the barn painting and adding some final touches before I can bring in the furniture. I want to wait until Bailey can help me pick out wall decor and other decorations so she feels at home, but I did buy a few books and some little knick knacks to go on her bookshelves as a surprise. I also made another set of bookends to match the ones I gave her a few months ago.

I had planned to reveal the cabin and barn to her on Friday night after dinner, but the evening didn't unfold exactly as expected. I also spent Saturday and Sunday with her, but I never felt the opportune moment had arrived.

Moreover, I had just shared the news that I had not only taken space from my family, but quit my job and sold my condo. I understand I have more than enough time to tell her, and I didn't want to overwhelm her with all that news at once. I want her to approach this opportunity with a positive mindset.

It's almost one o'clock when I decide to take a break and check my phone. I've missed three calls from Bailey in the past fifteen minutes. That's strange. She had mentioned that she had a few errands to run in the next town over and that she'd meet me at my place later this evening. I tap on her name to call her back.

"Mr. Sterling?" A calm but unfamiliar male voice comes through the other line. "Yes? Who is this?" I ask firmly.

"I'm sorry to do this over the phone," My heart beats fast and I suck in a breath assuming the worst. "I'm a doctor here at Denver UCHealth Hospital-" Before he can finish speaking I'm racing to my truck.

"How bad and where can I find her?" I growl. Not patient enough to get any further details, I'm on a one track mind to get to her as quickly as humanly possible.

"She's on the 4th floor, room 407. She's stable right now but was asking for you."

"I'm on my way, I'll be there in three hours." I drop my phone into the cup holder and grip the steering wheel. I can feel a panic attack creeping in and all I can do is focus on the road ahead of me. Driving to Denver was a blur and I'm not even sure how I made it here in once piece. She was asking for me, and I needed to get to her.

As I'm driving, I do wish I had let the doctor tell me what was happening so I'm not left with thinking worst case scenarios. I wonder if her parents were contacted as well. I have yet to meet them, but I know they are nice people and have a close relationship with their children.

Once I reach the hospital I screech to a halt in front of the valet, and toss my keys at the guy standing at the podium. I don't stop to give my name, and when he calls out for me I ignore him and race through the front doors. There is an elevator straight ahead that I make a break for.

I navigate the 4th floor without even noticing the signs or any clues that could guide me to which department she's been admitted to. Once I reach the unit with the corresponding room number, I'm stopped at a check-in desk.

They were expecting me and only needed to see my ID to print a visitors pass before I could enter. Within minutes, a nurse in pink scrubs led me back through the double doors of the unit.

"She's stable, but sedated," The tall nurse with her blonde hair in a tight high ponytail tells me. "We gave her some medication to help her calm down and sleep, as well as hopefully stop labor."

I'm sorry, stop what? My feet refuse to move, and I stare off ahead of the nurse. Did I hear her right? She notices I'm no longer following and turns to face me. I must not have a very good poker face because she's walking up to me quietly now and with a soft tone and says, "Bailey and the baby are fine right now, Mr. Sterling," She cannot be talking about my Bailey, right? There's got to be a mix up. My eyes begin to dart between the nurse and the room numbers around us to see if I can spot hers.

"She's twenty weeks and the chances of her miscarrying are low, but there were complications during the amniocentesis and she lost a lot of amniotic fluid. The baby was in distress and she began bleeding. Thankfully her OBGYN acted quickly and had her flown to us within 30 minutes," She places her hand on my shoulder and looks me in the eyes. "The flight crew was able to stabilize her before she even landed, and we have really high hopes that they will both be alright. Now let's go see your girl, ok?" With that she leads me down the hall and around the corner.

Next to a nurse's station and a large window overlooking the hospital courtyard, I can now see her behind two imposing glass doors. She lies in a hospital bed, with various machines connected to her and some bands around her abdomen that are visible. Her gown only covers her breasts, while a blanket covers her lower half. I'm in disbelief, yet it is her. And she is all alone.

Sitting next to her now, the nurse who brought me in is explaining the equipment she's connected to. Bailey is receiving oxygen support, and her belly bands are called an NST, short for non-stress test. They're monitoring the babies' vital signs with this device. I ask if she can perform an ultrasound to ease my nerves. Fortunately, she entertains my inquiry, and before I know it, I'm staring up at a screen displaying a tiny human, and I can hear its heartbeat. This baby is mine, mine and Bailey's and it's perfect. I've never felt more love for another human than I do right now, gazing at both of them.

Now that the nurse has left the room, and I have a sonogram photo she printed out for me in my hands, my panic slowly starts to disappear. And all I feel now is love and gratitude, and maybe a little bit of extreme exhaustion.

Stroking Bailey's hair and kissing her cheek I whisper, "You've done such a good job, Baby. I'm so proud of you both. Keep fighting."

I went through Bailey's phone to find her parent's phone numbers and call them. It only took about twenty minutes before her entire family was in the waiting room. I met them there to explain the little that I understood and was privy to. This isn't how I wanted to find out I was going to be a father, and I know this is not how they wanted to find out they were going to be grandparents, and an uncle and aunt.

Their main concern was Bailey's wellbeing, which is completely understandable, and I don't fault them for not really wanting to get invested in the idea of, or attached to a baby that may not survive. Especially since the baby was created with a guy they just met and had no idea existed in the first place.

Her mother was sobbing and holding tightly to her father's shirt. Her hair long and black, her eyes a rich blue like Bailey's, and just like Bailey I assume they are brighter when she's upset. She's wearing a top covered in paint, which matches my jeans that are also covered in paint. Neither one of us had a chance to change clothes before racing over here.

Only three people were allowed in at a time. her parents and Alec went in first while I stayed with Becca in the waiting room. She's a nurse and was trying to comfort me and give me her professional opinion on the situation. She was calm and reassuring, and had a warm smile and bubbly aura about her that put me at ease again.

Once her father, Bradley, felt comfortable enough with the state his daughter was in, and was able to see her for himself, he switched places with Becca so she could go in to be with Alec and Dana.

"I don't know who you are, or how long you've been seeing my daughter," standing eye to eye, I'm expecting him to chew my ass out and tell me to leave. "But I'm thankful you were here, and appreciate that you called us as soon as you could." He goes to shake my hand. His hair a rich brown like Baileys, with pepper of grey mixed in, and he's about my height but with a good 50 pounds on me. He could easily pummel me, and I'm really glad he chose the other route.

"Of course, sir. I know the circumstances aren't great, but I am not leaving her side. Respectfully, I love your daughter and the baby she is carrying is mine. I'm not going anywhere, and I'm glad you're here as well."

He nods in acceptance and drops his hand as he makes his way to the chairs seated in front of the check-in desk. We wait for a few minutes before Alec and Becca make their way to the front.

"We need to head out, but let us know if anything changes. Anything at all, good or bad." The three shake and hug goodbye, and it sends a tinge of jealousy through my body.

Bradley and I return to the room to be with Dana and Bailey. We all unanimously decide to stay here until she's released, and I call Aspen to inform her about the situation and persuade her to remain in Elk Hollow. Initially, she was disappointed that I suggested she stay, but she understands that Echo will be lonely and it would be more beneficial to us if she stayed there, taking care of her.

My adrenaline had been keeping me upright for most of the day, but now my nerves are shot and I feel a crash coming. There are two chairs and a pull out couch in the room. Her mother takes the cot, her father takes the recliner, and I take the most uncomfortable chair I have ever sat in and pull it up to her bed. I reach out for her hand and as soon as I lay my head down on her stomach, my body forces me into sleep.

Chapter Thirty-Four

BAILEY

I wake to the sound of an alarm blaring. "No, it's too early, let me sleep in." I groan in protest. "Bailey? You're okay, just calm down the nurse is coming." Rylan? Why is Rylan talking to me about a nurse? Is Becca on her way over for some reason? My eyes flutter open and I'm greeted with a rush of nurses, Rylan, and my parents all standing around my bed. Where the hell am I? I don't think we're in Kansas anymore, Toto.

Thankfully, a very vital cord had come undone, which is why a fleet of nurses had rushed into my room like there was a fire. It's not long before the room stills again though and I'm left alone with a frantic mother, stressed out father, and terrifying looking Rylan. I don't think I've ever seen the look on his face that he's currently wearing before. Not even around his family, which scares me. I take it they know. And now I need to face the music.

Wait. Fuck, I'm in the hospital, I'm pregnant and I'm in the hospital. "The baby?" I shout, placing my hand on my stomach and sitting up to look for anyone to answer me. "How is the baby? Someone tell me right now."

Rylan begins to walk over to me, his face unchanged but his demeanor calm. He sits on the edge of the bed where the safety bar is down and brushes my hair from my eyes. "The baby is fine, and so are you. There were complications and you were flown to Denver. They just want to keep you for observation for a few days."

I let out a sigh of relief and feel hot tears running down my cheeks. "I'm so sorry, I didn't plan to hide this from you."

"I know, baby. It's okay," He says as he kisses my forehead. I actually believe him. I don't think he's mad at me, but I can see how hurt he is. He's disappointed, scared, and frustrated. Honestly, that's so much worse than mad.

My parents walk over to the bed as Rylan goes to get up. "I"m going to give you a minute with your folks. I gotta find my truck and get some coffee. Let me know if anyone wants anything." And with that, he grabs his black zip up carhartt jacket from the back of the chair and I'm left to explain myself to them, alone.

They were also feeling everything I could see in Rylan, and like Rylan, I could see the love for me is outweighing the anger they are feeling.

The nurse came in and did an ultrasound for us to help me feel more at ease, and to help them feel more connected. She even printed out copies for them which I just know are going straight onto their refrigerator like the proud Grandparents I've always pictured them to be. However when I pictured them that way before, it was always with Alec and Becca's baby, not mine.

Whatever drugs they had me on were making me groggy, and I drifted back to sleep for a few hours after giving my parents the short version of everything that's been going on. Rylan was still gone when I fell asleep, but had called my room earlier to made sure we were doing alright. My dad said Rylan just needed some space, and to give him time to process and calm down.

Rylan

Fuck! I have no idea what I'm doing. I didn't want to leave Bailey at the hospital, but I had to get the fuck out of there to breathe, and I knew her parents wouldn't leave her side.

I plug my phone into the charger inside my truck and head to the nearest drive-thru coffee shop. This morning, I sent a text to Aspen, informing her that both Bailey and the baby are safe. Now, I need to call someone to calm me down before I have another panic attack. It won't be my family, despite my sudden desire to hear their voices. I decide to call Callum; he's essentially my brother anyway. The phone rings twice before he picks up, even though it's only six in the morning here.

"Hey, what's up man?" Callum is always so chill and reserved, I'm hoping that will be a good contrast to how I'm feeling right now, and he'll be able to mellow me out.

"I need to tell you something, and I need you to be open about it and not freak out cause I'm already doing enough of that. Can you do that?"

"Damn, bro. What happened?"

I proceed to lay everything out for him, and by the time I'm finished I'm in tears, finally processing what happened.

"Fuck man, I love her and this baby so damn much already, but I'm so hurt that she kept this from me, and I am so mad that I could have lost both of them without even knowing one of them existed." I'm pacing outside of my truck in an empty parking lot now. It's only thirty degrees outside, but I feel like my skin is on fire.

"Damn, Ry, that's incredibly challenging. First and foremost, I'm glad both of them are doing well. Secondly, congratulations! Thirdly, I could sense how much you care for Bailey even when I first saw you with her. I have no doubt that you'll be the best husband and father to them."

I stop in my tracks, that's the first time I've heard the word father out loud to describe me and it feels-incredible.

"You know, she was probably just really afraid you were going to dip out again. And time just got away from her and she became overwhelmed. That's my best guess."

"You're probably right-" I shiver. "So what do you think I should do now?" My internal temperature must have dropped because now I'm feeling the chill of the wind through to my bones. I hop back into my truck to drink some of my now lukewarm coffee, and hear him out.

"Well, calm your ass down, get back into that hospital, and just be there for her. Don't trauma dump all over her now, wait until you're both calm, and she's home and healthy." Callum was right, as always.

"Thanks man, I'll call you once we're home and let you know how we're doing."

We hang up and I'm feeling so much better. Before I head back to the hospital I stop into a store for a few items to bring back with me.

Bailey

The sun is peaking through the blinds of my hospital room when I wake up again. This time my parents are no longer in the room, and Rylan is sitting on the recliner next to the window in the corner of the room, leaning forward with his face in his hands.

"Rylan?" I say quietly to let him know that I'm awake. He sits up instantly and rushes over to me.

"How are you feeling? Do you need anything, the nurse? Water?" He's already at my bedside and pushing my hair back from my forehead. I love when he does that.

"No, I'm okay. Are you okay?" I almost don't want to know the answer, because I wouldn't be if I was in his position.

"I'll be fine once you're home with me. The doctor said you can be discharged tomorrow, but you're being put on temporary bedrest." His eyes are avoiding mine, it's like he's looking right through me even though he's right in front of me. Did I break him?

"Good, I'm ready to be in a real bed, and to see Echo. Oh my gosh! Echo-"

"Is fine, Aspen has her and she will be at the house waiting for us when we get back tomorrow."

My hands slide up to rest on my stomach and I smile. "Did you see the baby?" I ask him with a soft voice.

He reaches into his back pocket and pulls out his wallet, revealing a sonogram photo he had tucked into the back. "He, or she, is perfect."

I can see the love in his eyes and all my fears melt away. Regardless of how he feels towards me, I know he loves this baby just as much as I do, and that's all I could hope for.

He stands and pulls a bag out from behind the chair he was sitting in.

"I stopped by the grocery store and found these," He says handing the bag to me. "I hope you like them."

I open the grocery bag to see a small stuffed arctic fox, it instantly reminds me of Echo. And underneath the stuffed animal, a baby onesie. The onesie reads "Mommy Loves Me."

Instantly I'm crying, holding the onesie up to my heart.

"Can you please bring me my bag?"

The onesie I bought for him is buried at the bottom, I reach in and hand it to him. His eyes flutter as he reads the words across the shirt, "I Love My Daddy" he says with tears in his eyes now, too. "Great minds think alike."

He climbs onto the bed with me, laying sideways and places his hand over my stomach, gently stroking it with his thumb.

"I've never been more terrified than I was when I got the phone call telling me you were in the hospital," He glances at me now, our heads sharing the pillow. "You are my forever. If I lost you-."

"You won't lose me, Rylan. We have too much life to live together. The three of us."

Chapter Thirty-Five

RYLAN

B ailey has been home on bed rest for the past six weeks now, and has surprisingly been very cooperative and accepting of my help while she's out of commission. I don't doubt that she'll be a good mother, she already is.

Callum flew out to help me finish the final touches on the barn, including a new area I had added to the plans once we got back from the hospital. The cabin is almost finished as well, at this rate, it'll be finished before the baby gets here.

Juniper, Aspen, and Sandy have all been taking turns keeping Bailey company while I've been busy so she doesn't lose her mind, and the group even moved the bookclub to Bailey's house for now. They say it takes a village, and we have one.

Once Bailey comes off bed rest in a few weeks, I'll be driving her out to the property to show her what I've been working on for us.

I had been feeling bad keeping this secret from her, but then I'm reminded she hid our whole ass child from me for four months, and the feeling of guilt leaves pretty quickly. Not like I believe our relationship should continue to have secrets by any means, but this one isn't going to send her off the edge. I hope.

There is no doubt in my mind that I will marry this woman. I don't care when or how, but it will happen. She has become my everything, and I plan to ask her when we're at the cabin. I asked Aspen to come along with me to pick out a ring last week, and together we found the perfect one for Bailey. It's low profile, pear shaped diamond ring with 14 karat white gold. I also had the jeweler engrave a sunflower on the outside of the band, it's her favorite flower and it makes the ring even more personalized and special which I know she'll appreciate.

"I've got you, watch your step," Bailey is ridiculously clumsy, and pregnant. Maybe blindfolding her while we navigate a dirt path wasn't my smartest choice. I've got a pretty good grip on her, but knowing her, she'd trip on nothing and find a way to drag us both down.

"I have to pee, your child is kicking my bladder." Uh oh, that means I've got a maximum of five minutes to get her to a bathroom before she unleashes. Looks like I'll be rushing things.

"Alright, you can look now!" We're standing in front of the finished barn. It's exactly how I pictured, with my shop on the main floor, thankfully equipped with it's own plumbing and bathroom, and the stairs leading up the apartment is finished and has it's own entrance.

"Oh my God, Rylan! It's beautiful. How did you?-" She's crying now. I've gotten used to her hormones causing her to be a little extra emotional now, but I can tell she probably would've had this reaction even if she wasn't pregnant.

Once we make our way through the shop and up to the loft, she begins to take everything in. Wide eyed and tearful, she walks towards the bedroom area. The crib I built is beside the bed, and the bookcase has an additional area with baby books, some toys, and stuffed animals. Her fingers trail the railing of the crib while one hand rests on her stomach. "It's perfect, you're perfect." Her eyes flutter.

We're hoping to get the cabin finished before the baby comes, and not even need to use the apartment at all. But if that doesn't happen, I'm so thankful she appears to love it, and it makes me feel better to know that if I can't complete the house in time, she'd be happy here.

As I continue to walk Bailey through, our friends and family arrive to the property, preparing for her surprise engagement party. We are all that confident that she'll say yes. I invited my parents when I called to tell them about the baby, but they wanted no part in this "mistake." Kyle and Rachel must agree with them, because I haven't heard from them either. That's okay, I'm better off without them. The family that I've created with Bailey, our child, and our friends is the only family I need.

Once we are finished up with the apartment, she uses the restroom in the shop again. Before she comes out, I position myself in front of the barn doors with a bouquet of sunflowers, and get down on one knee. I'm shaking, I feel a panic attack come on, but not because I doubt my choice, but because

I've never loved anyone this much before. I see her step out of the office, she doesn't notice me right away.

"Bailey," Her eyes search for a few seconds before landing on mine. Covering her mouth, she begins to cry. "Rylan?" Holding one hand out for hers, she makes her way to me and places her hand in mine.

"I have been intrigued by you from the moment you threw a ball at me, I knew I was falling for you the moment you calmed me from my panic attack. When I saw you in that dress at Callum's, I had no doubt I wanted to see you in a white dress, walking down an aisle to meet me at the alter. And when I found out you were having my child, I realized I couldn't put it off any longer. I feel like my soul has yearned for yours from the moment they were intertwined," Tears streaming down her face, while my eyes threaten to do the same, I set the flowers down and pull the box from my pocket.

"Bailey Brynn Collins, will you marry me?"

"Yes! Yes! A million times over, yes!" She screams, holding her hand out for me to place the ring. Not even seconds pass and an eruption of cheering bursts from outside of the barn. She glances up as Aspen and Juniper rip open the doors and tear through the entrance, heading straight for her. Everyone is filing in one after another, making the rounds hugging and hand shaking to congratulate us. I've never seen her more happy and glowing than in this moment.

We married on March 5th, it was a small ceremony, perfect in every way. Bailey wanted to have a bigger wedding, but she was starting to feel the affects of the 3rd trimester, and neither one of us wanted to wait any longer to make it official. My best friend Cal got ordained online and married us, with our friends and her parents present. She was beautiful, and all mine. Bailey is officially my wife. Fuck, *my wife*. I can't stop saying it and sometimes I can't believe it.

With the help of all of our friends and her family, we managed to finish the house and moved into it. Everyone wanted us to be settled in before the baby came, and her parents wanted the barn apartment to be available for them to stay with us for a few weeks.

The nursery is decorated, and in the room down the hall from ours. I'm nervous having it so far from us, but I was able to convince Bailey to put the crib in our room for now.

Everything is coming together just as I had imagined it would. I can picture us raising our children here, growing old together here. Nestled between the trees, up on a hill overlooking Elk Hollow. It's quiet and absolutely perfect.

It's now mid- April, and we're currently in the hospital preparing to meet our first child.

Bailey's been having contractions since last night, and I'm pretty sure I broke a couple of laws getting us here as quickly as possible.

I'm absolutely freaking out, will I be a good father? Can I do this? Will the kid even like me? A million thoughts running through my head when suddenly I hear the doctor say "Okay dad, it's time."

She's having a c section, which is terrifying for both of us, but the doctor let us know this is the safest choice for both of them.

I'm positioned up by her head, stroking her hair and holding her hand.

"You've got this baby, you're doing so good. I'm so proud of you."

I lean in to kiss her when we suddenly the room is filled with a gentle crying, "It's a girl!" The doctor shouts from behind the curtain, holding her up to us.

I can't see very much through my tears, but I can hear our daughter and it's the most amazing sound.

Once they do a few things, they wrap her up and place her on Bailey's chest. We're allowed to hold her for a few minutes before they take her to the recovery area. Bailey grabs my arm, "Don't leave her side. I'll be there soon, I love you."

As much as I didn't want to leave her, my soul was splitting in two, and the half that needed me more was leaving the room, and I felt the pull to follow. I kissed Bailey, stroked her hair again, and told her how proud of her I was.

I thought marrying her was the best moment of my life, but this, this is something else. This is something indescribable.

Once Bailey and I are back in our room with our daughter, they give her some pains meds to help her get some sleep. She's been awake for over thirty-six hours, and her body needs rest so she can begin to recover from surgery.

Our daughter begins to stir, so I walk over to her cot that's next to Bailey's bed, pick her up and bring her to the rocking chair with me. I can't look away, she's breathtaking. She has her mothers lips and ears, and I'm in love.

I rock her for hours, humming to her until it's time for Bailey to wake up to feed her again.

I feel like my life has truly just begun, and I have never felt more peace than I do right now in this moment.

Braylynn Ady Sterling was born April 13th, at 4:03 pm. It's now mid- May, and I have been her father for an entire month now.

It feels like just yesterday we brought her home. So tiny, so fragile. Though we may be sleep deprived, this past month has been full of absolute bliss. Every doubt I had about becoming a father has vanished. I know I will never be like mine. I will give my daughter the world, and never let her feel like she's not worthy of any bit of it.

I had to head to Denver for a few supplies, the rain is coming down hard, and it's dark now. I'm only 40 minutes away from home, but I have an aching feeling in my chest, something pulling at me, telling me that I need to get home to my girls.

I give them a quick call, but there's no answer so I leave a voicemail. "Hey Bailey Boo, just checking in on you and Braylee girl. I love you both so much, see you soon."

The roads are winding, and slippery. I'm in my truck though so I'm not too worried. Just as I begin to calm, something darts out in front of me. I swerve, trying to avoid hitting it, and my truck begins to roll.

I've got to get back to my girls– my girls.

Chapter Thirty-Six

BAILEY

Rylan Caine Sterling died on May 13th, at 9:03 pm.

The service was beautiful. Heartbreaking and beautiful. His parents didn't show, but I didn't expect them to after everything. Tasha and Mikey came of course, and Kyle sent a card; but I'm pretty sure it was his secretary that had sent it. What a fucking coward.

Callum and Juniper have been here since the day after the accident. They are staying in the barn apartment for now, and something tells me they aren't planning on leaving any time soon, if ever.

I appreciate everyone stepping in to help. Grieving the loss of Rylan, while holding our beautiful daughter is a strange feeling.

On one hand, when I look at her, I feel an immense amount of pride, joy, and love. But she looks just like him. She's a part of him and he isn't here with us to watch her grow, and that pain is unbearable.

I haven't slept in the room we shared since he died. The bed still smells like him and I don't want it to be disrupted. I'm not ready for that.

The first night without him, I couldn't breathe. Aspen and Micah stayed in Braylynn's nursery with her, and I sat in the master bathroom shower with the water flowing over me for hours; remembering the night I sat with him at his condo back in Dallas all those months ago. Wishing he were here to comfort me now, and not feeling him anywhere.

Braylynn is the only reason I kept going. My daughter, *our* daughter, needed me.

It's been three months since I had kissed Rylan goodbye for the final time, the feeling of his lips on mine still burned into my memory.

I'm angry, downright furious at the world. How dare it give him to me and then rip him away?

I replay his final voicemail often, it's backed up in four different places so I never lose it. Something tells me he knew what was coming, he knew he wasn't going to make it home to us.

I'm thankful he didn't sound afraid, but that he felt the need to call me and leave that message. Why couldn't I have just answered the fucking phone? I don't even remember what I was doing when he called, or why I didn't have my phone with me. I will never forgive myself for that. The only upside is that if I had answered, I wouldn't have the voicemail, and I might have heard pass. I just hope he wasn't afraid.

Braylee girl is turning three today, her auburn locks are curled at the ends; she looks more like Rylan every day. I get lost looking into her eyes, just like I had done with his years ago. She's such a happy girl, she doesn't have the pain of losing him like I do. She's surrounded by our friends. They came when we needed them the most, and I ever left. I've never had to walk this journey truly alone.

I wasn't expecting this, but I've found love with someone else, someone that also knew Rylan and knew how special he was. He doesn't ask me to forget him, and he's patient with me as I navigate life as a widow and mother to a young child. He's kind, and shares memories of Rylan with me, and talks to Braylynn about him, too.

I know Rylan would want me to move forward, to be happy. And I know he would approve of the man I'm finding myself opening up to, but I can't help but feel guilty some days.

Rylan was cremated and sits on the mantle with a photo of the three of us. There's photos of him throughout the house, but this is my favorite, as it's the only one of us as a family of three.

Though he was cremated, there's a headstone for him at the town cemetery, with a bench next to it. Before Braylynn's party, I had to run into town to pick up her cake, and something pulled me to visit the site before heading home.

I make my way through the cemetery, being careful not to disturb any of the surrounding plots or patrons. There are a few families here today, and I keep my eyes down to give them privacy, but being aware of their presence.

As I approach Rylan's headstone, something catches my eye. As it comes into view, I finally realize what I'm seeing, and it almost brings me to my knees. It's a single sunflower. I glance around, checking for more around other headstones. Curious if a good samaritan left these for others. No, this is the only one. It's not just propped up against his headstone, it's actually growing from the ground beneath. Instantly I realize who it's from, and a tear falls from my face.

Rylan. I breathe in, closing my eyes, letting the sun hit my face, my body is filled with a warmth that has been absent for so long now. I feel you, I love you.

I take another deep breath, kiss my fingers and place my hand onto his headstone. I begin to walk away but before I do, I turn to face his memorial once again.

"Your girls are going to be okay."

Epilogue

BRAYLYNN

Braylynn, Age 5

My mommy has tons of photos of my Daddy, but my favorites are the ones with me and him together. There aren't many of those though, he died soon after I was born. The best thing she has, is a video of me and Daddy the day I came home from the hospital.

"Welcome home baby girl," He says holding me as he walks through the front door. He looks scared, like he's worried he's going to drop me. But he also looks really happy, I like to think it's because I'm his princess and Mommy is his Queen and we saved him.

The video isn't very long, but he holds me the entire time, walking me through our new house he built for us, showing me around even though my eyes are closed, silly Daddy. We still live here, and I love it. I have tons of space to run and play, and I have a bunch of toys. I even have a lot of my family living here! After Daddy died, I guess everyone came to help Mommy, and no one left! They must really love me.

Auntie Tash, Auntie Junie, and Auntie Aspen are my best friends, they love to do my hair and dance with me. Uncle Mikey, Uncle Cal, and Uncle Micah are always here to make sure I'm safe and what mommy calls spoiled? But she says it with a smile, so I don't think it's a bad thing!

Everyone tells me I have Daddy's eyes, and laugh. I wish I could hear his laugh. When I'm feeling sad and miss him, I squeeze my fox stuffy I've had since I was a baby. I'm very careful with it, it's from Daddy, and I know I can't get another just like it if something happens to it.

Braylynn, Age 9

I knew watching mommy get remarried was going to be tough. I don't remember my daddy much, but he lives through those that loved and knew him, and his memory has never been forgotten. Everyone talks about him a lot.

I don't know why I'm so sad today, I love Conner. He's not my real dad, but he treats us really well and loves us. He knew my daddy, they were friends. Not super close like daddy and Uncle Callum, but he started coming around after he met us at the funeral. He stayed to help Uncle Cal build the house for him and Aunt Junie next to ours. Then he stayed to build the rest of the cabins for my other aunts and uncles who wanted to stay here, too.

Conner and my mom have been dating for years, so I'm not surprised they are getting married. And I am happy for them, I'm just sad Daddy isn't here. Conner promised me he isn't trying to take my Daddy's place, and I believe him. I hope Daddy isn't sad that Conner is marrying Mommy.

Braylynn, Age 16

"He did what?" Yells Uncle Callum, storming down the hallway. It's not long before my uncles are rushing through my bedroom door, all three of them. I take it my mom and dad told them about Zachary. He's the boy I've been dating since 8th grade, and he broke up with me last night in front of everyone at my friends party. Then I saw him kissing my friend Aly before I left. I've never felt heartbreak like this before. I wanted to punch him, and her!

My Uncles are extremely protective over me, always have been. I know I'm lucky to have them. I think they've felt a sense of responsibility to me since Dad couldn't be here. Conner is a really great step father, he's never let me down, and is always so supportive of me and mom. She even opened her own coffee shop a few years ago with his help, and he put his own business aside so she could focus on hers.

"Want me to beat him up?" Callum says pacing back and forth.

"He's a teenager," Uncle Mikey says hitting Cal in the arm.

"Can't we just hire another kid to beat him up for us?" Quips Uncle Micah, leaning up against the wall with his arms crossed.

They all have children of their own now, but somehow they all managed to only produce boys. I'm the only girl, which keeps them just as protective of me as they were before.

"C'mon guys, out of her room. I didn't tell you about it so you could threaten to beat a kid up or bombard her," my dad says, pushing past Uncle Cal and kicking them out.

Once everyone takes turns to lean down to kiss my head and hug me goodbye, they all file out as he sits on the edge of my bed. "Hey princess, sorry about them. They mean well."

"I know, dad. Thanks."

"Your mother and I are going to take your brother into town for some ice cream in a bit, wanna come?"

My brother Peyton is seven, and he's super annoying and feral; he loves to follow me everywhere. Mom had a rough pregnancy and delivery with Peyton. She agreed not to have anymore children after him and had her tubes tied. I guess the pregnancy with me was really scary, too. She says we're the best things that have ever happened to her though and she wouldn't change a thing. She has a piece of Daddy in me, and a piece of Conner in Peyton.

I take after Daddy in so many ways, especially in looks. I share his golden eyes; which used to make my mom really sad when she looked into them. She would never admit it to me though, but I could tell.

The only things I share physically with mom is my height, and my dimples. Peyton has moms eyes, they are bright blue like hers. Otherwise he's a mini Conner, and already showing signs he's going to be really tall like him, too.

"Yeah, that sounds nice," I say as dad pulls me into a hug.

Braylynn, Age 25

"I'm scared as shit, why am I so nervous?" My palms are sweating, and I have to keep rubbing them against my jeans to get the sticky feeling off. It's hot here, I don't like it.

"It's completely understandable," Says Peyton on the other end of the phone. "I wish you would've let me come with you, though." He's sixteen now, and just as over protective as our Uncles are for me, even though I'm a whole adult now, and he's still just a kid. A kid that towers over me. I'm only 5'5" like mom, but Peyton stands at 6 foot now, and looks like a grown ass man.

"You have school, sorry Peyton. But thanks. I'll call you as soon as I'm back at my hotel. Love ya!" I hang up and stare ahead at the huge house in front of me. It's springtime and I swear it's hotter here in spring than it ever reaches in Elk Hollow during the summertime. I don't like Texas, and I'm pretty sure I'll never come back.

Heading up to the steps, I can see some people through the window. They are expecting me, I sent a letter. I ring the doorbell in anticipation and stand back, not sure what to expect.

The door opens and I'm greeted by an older woman, somewhere in her seventies, standing behind her is a man with peppered dark brown and grey hair. The woman is crying and holding her arms out to me, "Oh my goodness, you look so much like my Rylan." She says. The man behind her has one hand on her back, and extends the other out to me for a handshake.

"I'm your uncle Kyle, this is your Grandmother, Patricia. Come on in, my sister, brother in law, and your cousins are waiting to meet you."

I step in as they close the door behind me. There are photos of my father and the rest of his family on the wall, and there's a large portrait of my dad with his father that had passed a few years ago in the dining room. They say Aunt Natasha painted it shortly after Grandpa died. We have one in our house she painted of just Dad, it's one of my favorites. She also made me a small one for my sixteenth birthday of me and him together, since I can't have photos of us, it's the next best thing.

I stay for a few hours, listening to stories of his childhood, and how sorry they were about how everything unfolded. They regret pushing him and my mother away, because it also meant I wasn't apart of their lives. But they are happy they got to meet me now, and hope to see me again soon.

I leave feeling satisfied, knowing I wouldn't have forgiven myself if I hadn't come here to meet them, but I also know that I have everything and everyone I need already. My mom and dad, as well as my aunts and uncles, made sure of it.

I don't feel the need to ever return to the Sterling house, my dad's presence isn't here. It's home, at the cabin he built on a hill, just outside of Elk Hollow, with mom. Unbeknownst to him, he constructed this to last.

THE END

Acknowledgements

First and foremost, I'd like to thank my son for putting up with his mommy being on the computer day and night, and for being supportive of me and my hobby. You were the reason I pushed so hard to complete and publish this. I wanted to show you that as long as you have a passion and work hard, you can do anything you set your mind to. Please, always remember to follow your heart, and chase your dreams. I love you forever and always, to the moon and back, to infinity and beyond. But also, please skip chapters 5, 6, 12, 15, 16, 20, 24, 31 if you're going to read this someday. KThanks.

Next, I'd like to thank my Mamma, Michelle. You have always been so supportive of anything I choose to do in life, and you've always had faith in my writing capabilities. When my laptop died, you offered to pay for half of the cost of a new one same day, so I wouldn't have a delay in writing, and you saw it as an investment in my future. You're the real MVP for that. Thank you for always being on my team, and for reading this even if it's awkward, I love you!

A special thank you to my cousin, best friend, editor, beta reader, and hype man, Adylene, for always putting up with me and my never-ending bullshit. I couldn't have done this without you or the little crocheted sunflower I keep by my laptop that you bought for me. Your support for me in all things, but especially this, has never wavered. I am so incredibly thankful to have you in my life, and I can't wait to sign your copy. I love you, always.

To my Papa, Robert. When I let you know I was in the process of writing a novel that I had every intention on publishing, you didn't share concerns or criticism, just support and love. Thank you for everything you've done for me growing up, and even now.

To my Grandma, Sandra. Though you are not with us anymore, your love for reading and talent for writing is with me, and I feel your presence through our shared love and passions.

To my extended family, I know I can do anything with your support and love, thank you for always being here for me and my son.

To my friends, I know I've been a shit-tastic friend (at best) this past year give or take, and I appreciate your understanding and support.

To my fur baby Echo Keikoa, I know you can't read, but thank you for being my buddy and always being near while I write.

Afterword

Thank you to my readers and followers. Every book purchased, every page read, and every download to your e-reader supports me and my dream to become an author full time.

All reviews are welcomed and appreciated, even if this wasn't your cup of tea. I know this genre isn't for everyone, and as a debut author, I have a lot to learn. There's always room to grow. Thank you for taking the time to read, and leaving a review. Love you all!

I really struggled with how to end their story the further along I got. I thought I had it all figured out before I even started writing, but Rylan had other plans. I understand that it was a huge risk for me to take, pulling a Nicholas Sparks as my editor and I would call it, but it had to happen. I'm sorry for any tears that were shed in Rylan's name. Please forgive me.

Thank you to Rylan and Bailey for living in my head, and for giving me my first completed story. I hope I did you justice, and I hope others fall in love with you and your love story as much I did. If you'd like to see what I'm working on next, join my socials to get some sneak peaks!

I'm really excited for you to meet Silas in my upcoming dark romance.

He's a mysterious masked biker with tattoos, and has an affinity for making thirst traps and claiming and protecting what's his; no matter the cost.

Playlist

Euclid - Sleep Token
All Time Low - Jon Bellion
DYWTYLM - Sleep Token
Are You Really Okay? - Sleep Token
Dancing All Alone - Clinton Kane
The Love You Want - Sleep Token
Let Em Go - Matt Hansen
Fall For Me - Sleep Token
Walk This World With Me - The Home Team
Belong Together - Mark Ambor
Miles Away ft Kellin Quinn - Memphis May Fire
Without Me - Dayseeker
Lover - Taylor Swift
One Day You're Gone - Gavn!
Bigger Than The Whole Sky - Taylor Swift
Save You A Seat - Alex Warren

About the Author

Brianna is a mom in her early 30's to her son and deaf Australian Shepherd in Colorado. When she's not writing, she's reading or hanging out with her family and friends. Her favorite book genres are dark romance and romcoms and she has a strong relationship with iced coffee, even when it's snowing. She also loves post hardcore/rock music and getting & admiring tattoos.

www.ingramcontent.com/pod-product-compliance
Lightning Source LLC
Chambersburg PA
CBHW070742180626
46818CB00007B/2958